SIGHTWITCH

SIGHTWITCH

THE TRUE TALE OF THE TWELVE PALADINS

Susan Dennard

Illustrations by Rhys Davies

TOR TEEN

A TOM DOHERTY ASSOCIATES BOOK

New York

SIGHTWITCH

Copyright © 2018 by Susan Dennard

Illustrations by Rhys Davies

Map by Maxime Plasse

A Tor Teen Book
Published by Tom Doherty Associates
175 Fifth Avenue
New York, NY 10010

www.tor-forge.com

Tor® is a registered trademark of Macmillan Publishing Group, LLC.

The Library of Congress Cataloging-in-Publication
Data is available upon request.

ISBN 978-1-250-18352-1 (hardcover)
ISBN 978-1-250-19388-9 (international, sold outside
the U.S., subject to rights availability)
ISBN 978-1-250-18353-8 (ebook)

Our books may be purchased in bulk for promotional, educational, or business use. Please contact your local bookseller or the Macmillan Corporate and Premium Sales Department at 1-800-221-7945, extension 5442, or by email at MacmillanSpecialMarkets@macmillan.com.

First Edition: February 2018

Printed in the United States of America

0 9 8 7 6 5 4 3 2 1

FOR RACHEL

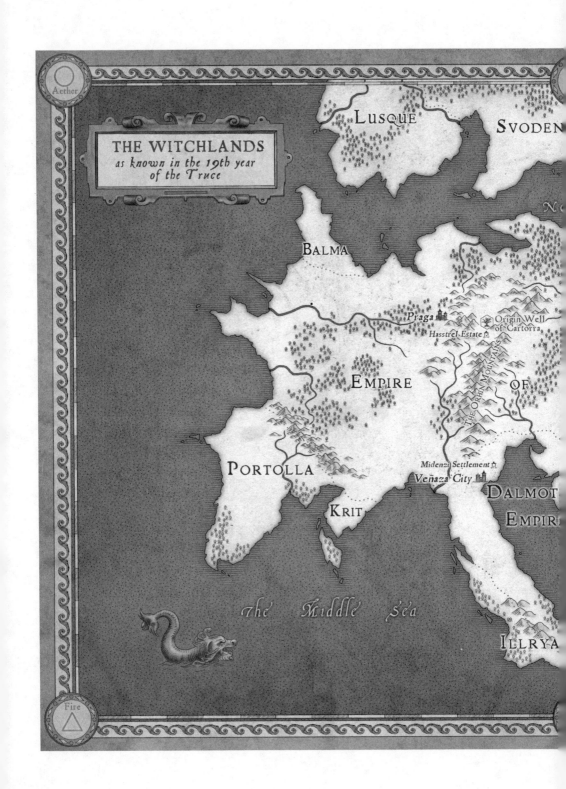

Æther

Fire

LUSQUE

SVODEN

THE WITCHLANDS
as known in the 19th year
of the Truce

BALMA

N

Praga
Hasstrel Estate

Origin Well
of Cartorra

EMPIRE

OF

THE ORHIN MOUNTAINS

Midenzi Settlement
Veñaza City

PORTOLLA

KRIT

DALMOT

EMPIR

ILLRYA

The Middle Sea

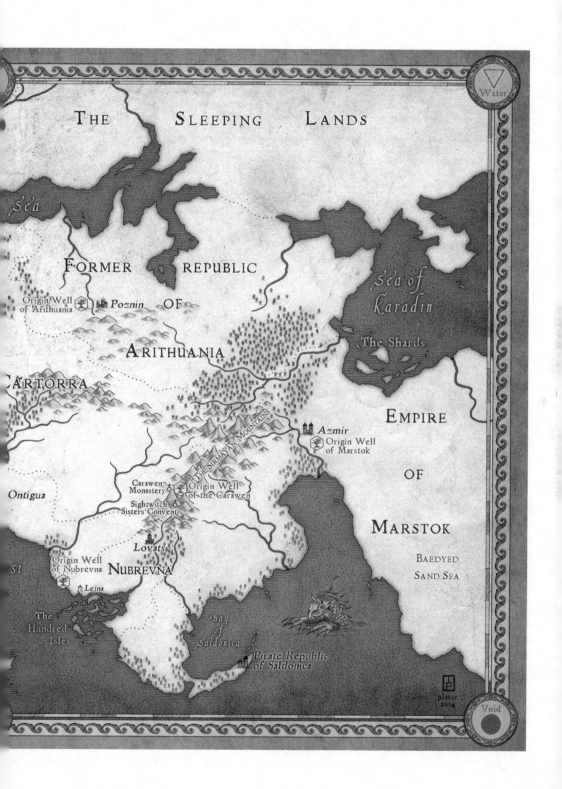

SIGHTWITCH

You don't remember me, do you, Kullen?

I'm familiar, though. When I walked into the Cleaved Man, you squinted your eyes as if there was something in my face you knew. Something that made you rub at the scar on your chest.

Don't you wonder how you got that scar?

Think, Kullen. The memories are in there. The spell that made you forget—it doesn't erase everything that happened. It simply buried the past, too deep for you to summon without help.

I'm here to help.

My name is Ryber Fortiza, but you, in your Nubrevnan conceit, misheard. You called me "Ryberta Fortsa." I called you "Captain."

My eyes were brown then. Not silver.

Take this book home. Read it from cover to cover—every page, every line. It has all you need to remember about what happened between us. It has all you need to learn.

That is to say . . . I think it does. I do not know entirely what you will find once you open it. Sightwitch diaries have a way of changing, depending on who read them. All I can say for certain is what I placed inside: records of when I found you, when I healed you, and when I hauled you into the depths of a mountain.

Read it, Kullen Ikray. Read it, and remember.

The Sleeping Giant

Said to always guide north, the Sleeping Giant is a cluster of three stars, visible even with the moon at its fullest.

Several theories exist for the origin of the constellation's name, many of which are rooted in different fables meant to keep children well-behaved. However, I posit that the name predates all of those fables as well as the cultures that created them.

Follow the Bat in the mountains, to find the soil and stones.
Follow the Fox and the Iris, to find the tides of home.
Follow the Hound and the Giant, to find the winds and the storm.
And follow the Hawk moving eastern, to find what flames have born.
Follow the Rook to the snowcaps, and you'll find the soul that begins.
But it's in the pitch-deep darkness, that you'll find where all things end.

**—Sightwitch Sister skipping song
to remember the constellations**

———— ✳ ————

Ryber Fortiza
Y18 D152

MEMORIES

Tanzi was summoned today.

It happened like it always does: we were at morning prayer in the observatory, hunched in our seats with eyes closed. I was sitting with the other Serving Sisters, a swathe of brown through the hall of silver Sightwitches. We might be all nationalities, all origins, all ages, but Serving Sisters always sat on one end. Full-fledged Sightwitch Sisters always sat on the other.

Clouds had gathered overnight. A flimsy light filtered through the

stained glass in the observatory's ceiling, casting the amphitheater rows in shadows.

We had just begun the Memory Vow. Head Sister Hilga stood beside the scrying pool at the room's heart, her hands clasped at her belly and her eyes closed. Our voices bounced on the marble walls, eighty-seven throats sounding like a thousand.

As the final words in the Memory Vow—"Once seen, never forgotten. Once heard, never lost"—crossed our lips, a telltale flap of wings echoed out.

My heart dropped to my toes, as it always does when I hear that sound.

Please be for me, I begged, staring at the stained-glass dome overhead—at the constellation of bright stars. *Please be coming for me, Sleeper. I follow all the Rules, I've learned all my lessons, and I have served you without complaint for thirteen years. Please, Sirmaya, Summon me.*

I wanted to vomit. I wanted to shout. Surely, surely my day had finally come.

Then the spirit swift appeared, swirling out of the scrying pool. A black mist that coalesced into a sharp-tailed, graceful-winged figure, its feathers speckled with starlight. It circled once, with eyes that glowed golden, and a wintery, crisp smell wafted over me.

That smell meant a Summoning.

Pick me, I prayed, the tips of my fingers numb from clutching so tightly at my tunic. *Pick me, pick me—*

The spirit swift twirled past the telescope ledge before winging down to the

PRAYERS
OF THE
SIGHTWITCH
SISTER

The Memory Vow

In the name of Sirmaya,
I vow to preserve
All that has come before,
For the past is the only truth.
Once seen, never forgotten.
Once heard, never lost.

The Vow of Clear Eyes

In the name of Sirmaya,
I vow to see
With clear eyes and open mind.
For the world is ever changing,
And the present is the
only constant.

The Vow of a Future Dreamed

In the name of Sirmaya,
I vow to protect
The future that is shown,
For the sleeper knows all
The sleeper dreams all,
And there is no changing
what is meant
to be.

Serving Sisters, fourteen of us in brown. I swayed. My heart surged into my throat.

Two hops. It was almost to me, if aiming slightly more toward Tanzi. But there was still a chance it might change course. Still a chance it might twist back to me . . .

It didn't. It skipped over to Tanzi's toes because, of course, the swift could not be here for me.

They are *never* here for me.

Seventeen years old, and my eyes are still their natural brown. Thirteen years at the Convent, and I'm still consigned to drab cotton.

Somehow, though, I managed to keep my throat from screaming, *No!* I wanted to shriek—Sirmaya knows I wanted to shriek and that my eyes burned with tears. It wasn't Tanzi's fault, though, that the Goddess had picked her first.

And it wasn't Tanzi's fault that our loving Goddess never seemed to want me at all.

If I was going to blame anyone, I should blame Sister Rose and Sister Gwen, Sister Hancine and Sister Lindou. All those years grow-ing up, they had filled my head with stories, telling me that I would be a powerful Sightwitch one day. That I would be the next Head Sister with a Sight to rival even Hilga's. No, they had never seen such visions, but they were sure of it all the same.

Why did I still cling to those old tales when they were so clearly not true? If the Sleeper had truly wanted to give me the strongest Sight, then surely She would have done so by now.

So I didn't cry and I didn't scream. Instead, I forced a smile to my lips and gave Tanzi a hug. She looked so worried, I couldn't *not* offer my Threadsister something. Her thick eyebrows had drawn into a single black line. Her russet skin was pinched with worry and guilt, an expression I never wanted to see on her face. If smiling would ease it, then smiling I could do.

"One of our ranks has been Summoned," Sister Hilga intoned. The words she always said, words that were never spoken for me. "Praise be to Sirmaya."

"Praise be to Sirmaya," the Sisters murmured back. Except for me. Tanzi still hugged me so tight, so fierce.

So afraid.

"You're not supposed to hug me," I whispered. Hilga was already walking toward us, the Summoning bell pulled from her belt.

"Forget the rules for one second," Tanzi hissed back. "And water my violets while I'm gone. Unless, of course, you get Summoned too."

"Yes." I held my smile as stiff as the stars in the stained glass. "Unless I get Summoned too."

Empty words made of dust. We both knew it would never happen. Summonings are rare enough; two Sisters Summoned at once is practically unheard of. And with each day that passes, the less I think I will *ever* get called inside the mountain to earn the gift of Sight.

Then that was it. That was all Tanzi and I got for a good-bye before my Threadsister was tugged onward and the rest of us were assembling into rows. At the end was me, all alone, for our number does not break evenly.

Hilga rang the bell once, and its bright tinkle filled the observatory. Filled my ears, then hooked deep into my heart and yanked down.

I hated the sound of that bell even more than the deeper bell that followed. The one in the belfry above the Crypts' Chapel.

At the main bell's single toll, we walked.

Little Trina, who is at least two hands shorter than I, glanced back at me. Pity clouded her blue eyes. Or maybe it wasn't pity but rather a fear that she'd one day end up like me: seventeen and still pall-eyed. Seventeen and still dressed in brown.

Seventeen and still un-Summoned by our sleeping Goddess, Sirmaya.

I pretended not to see Trina staring, and when we began the Chant of Sending, I hummed the hollow tones louder than I had ever hummed before. I wanted Tanzi to hear me, all the way at the front of the line, as we wound out of the observatory and up the trail into the evergreens.

Two of the Serving Sisters had cleared this path last week, but already white rubble clotted the pine-needle path. It sheds from the mountain each time she shakes herself.

I will have to clean it again tomorrow—just you wait. Hilga will come to me in the morning with that chore. Except this time, there will be no Tanzi to help.

When at last we reached the chapel pressed against the mountain's white face, the chant came to an end. Always the same rhythm, always the same timing.

We all stopped there, at the entrance into the Crypts, the Convent's vast underground library. The chant was over, but its memory still hung in the air around us as we fanned into half circles around the arched entrance.

The spirit swift that had Summoned Tanzi swooped over us now, briefly multiplying into three aetherial birds. Then six. Then shrinking back into one before sailing through the open door.

When it had disappeared from sight, Hilga nodded at Tanzi. "From this day on, Tanzi Lamanaya will be no more. She will leave us as a Serving Sister and return with the Gift of Clear Eyes."

"Praise be to the Sleeper," we all murmured—even me, though it made my stomach hurt to say it.

Tanzi smiled then. A brilliant, giddy one with no sign of her earlier fret.

And who could blame her? Even she, who waxed day in and day out about wanting to leave the Convent—even *she* wanted the Sight as badly as the rest of us.

And now she would get it. She'd been Summoned by the Sleeper, the most important moment in the life of a Sightwitch Sister. The only moment, really, that matters.

I tried to mimic her grin. Tried to show Tanzi that I was happy for her—because I was. A person can grieve for herself yet still revel in someone else's good fortune.

Our eyes barely had time to connect before Hilga gripped Tanzi's shoulder and turned her away.

They walked, Tanzi and Hilga, step by measured step into the chapel. Into the mountain. Soon enough, they were lost to the shadows.

The next time I would see Tanzi, her eyes would no longer match mine.

The other Sisters turned away then and marched back to the observatory in their perfect lines.

I lingered behind, my gaze trapped on the words etched into the marble above the chapel entrance.

TWO OR MORE AT ALL TIMES,

FOR A LONE SISTER IS LOST.

We call it the Order of Two, and no matter your heritage, the letters shift and melt into whatever language you find easiest to read.

For me, that is Cartorran. My aunt took me from Illrya before I was old enough to learn its written language.

I could not help but wonder, every time I saw these letters, *What do those words look like for someone who cannot read?*

I shook my head. A useless question, and one that left me running to catch back up to the group.

The rest of my day unfolded in silence.

Tanzi's half of the bed is cold now, as I write this. Only without her here do I realize how adapted to her presence I am. Her sideways snorts when she thinks something's funny. The constant cracking of her knuckles while she talks. Or even how she breathes heavy in her sleep, not quite a snore, but a sound I'm so accustomed to.

I don't want to sleep. I don't want to wake up alone. And I don't want to wake up wondering, yet again, why, why, *why* I am still without the Sight.

※

Tanzi Lamanaya

X10 D234

Today, I received a knife with an amber on the hilt. My mentor, Sister Hilga, told me it is the "key to the past" and that I must not lose it. "Every Sister at the Convent has their own key," she said. "And they are not to be shared."

She also gave me a huge book called *A Brief Guide to the Sight-witches* and this diary, in which I'm supposed to record all events of the day. Then, upon waking, I must record all of my dreams.

I hope I can remember my dreams. I've never remembered them before.

Today, I learned the hierarchy of the Sightwitch Sisters. I don't think I'll forget the three kinds of Sisters, seeing as I live here now and will be seeing them every day, but I also do not want to disobey my mentor. Especially since my roommate, a girl named Ryber Fortiza, has now scolded me twice for not following the rules.

Ryber is from Illrya, and she's just like Gran-Mi always said the Illryans were: focused and serious.

"Your bed is not made right," Ryber pointed out earlier. Then just a few moments later, she said, "You will get us into trouble, Tanzi. The lanterns are snuffed at the twenty-first chimes, and lighting a candle after that would be breaking Rule 33."

Her dark eyes have been narrowed ever since and her brow sloped so low. Gran-Mi would say that she has a face for telling stories, because it is so expressive.

I miss Gran-Mi. I hope I don't cry tonight. I don't think Ryber would like that.

Oh, no, Ryber is staring expectantly at me again. I had better write what I remember from my lessons.

First, we were assigned something called the Nine Star Puzzle. "Given the nine stars," Hilga said, "connect them all with only four lines and without lifting your chalk from the slate."

The nine stars were laid out like this:

But I still haven't figured out how to connect the stars with only four lines. And I've tried a hundred different ways.

After that, we learned the three kinds of Sisters.

Ryber drew the pictures for me and added the notes. She says it's better to have pictures in our diaries, but I can't draw.

"Not yet," Ryber told me, "but you'll learn." Then she read what I'd written about her above, and she laughed. A big sound. The kind Gran-Mi would've called "catching."

"You can call me Ry," she said next. "And I'm sorry I nagged you earlier. But Rule 8 says, 'Obedience is holy.' So you see? Only by following the Rules will Sirmaya know which Sisters are good enough for her to Summon."

also called "pall-eyes" because our vision is shrouded without the Sight

No one knows. "You'll understand when you're Summoned," is what Sister Hilga always tells me.

Serving Sisters are acolytes at the Convent. They serve the Sightwitch Sisters by helping to clean, cook, and garden.

Summoned Sisters are acolytes who have been Summoned by Sirmaya to go into the mountain. For up to two days, a Sister is underground meeting the Goddess, but I don't really know what that means.

Our eyes will turn silver!

This will be us one day!

Sightwitch Sisters have the Sight, meaning they can look at something once and remember it forever. They also can use their knives (like the knife Sister Hilga gave me) to remove memories from corpses. And, when they pray together, the Sisters can see visions in the scrying pool at the observatory.

"Oh," I said, thinking back to the massive list of Rules that Hilga had showed me earlier.

There were a lot.

Ry seemed to know what I was thinking because she laughed again and said, "Don't worry. You have time to learn it all. I've been here for five years—since I was four years old!—and I'm still learning."

Then she smiled big, and I smiled back.

"What about the Nine Star Puzzle?" I asked. "I haven't figured that out yet."

"Me either! And I've been trying to solve since I got here." She shrugged. "Sister Hilga says that it takes some Sisters their whole lives to find the answer."

I winced. "I hope it doesn't take *me* my whole life."

"It won't, Tanz. It won't." Ryber laughed after that, a bright sound that made me laugh too.

I like how she called me "Tanz."

"Do you have other questions?" she asked while neatly turning down her half of the bed.

I hesitated. I *did* have a question, but I did not want to be rude. My curiosity got the better of me in the end, though. "Why did Sister Lindou say I was lucky to share a room with you?"

"Oh." Ryber's face fell, and I knew right away I shouldn't have asked. I should have "practiced restraint" like Gran-Mi always taught me.

"They tell me I will have strong Sight one day," Ryber answered eventually. "Stronger than other Sisters. So I guess being with me is . . . special."

I wanted to ask her why her Sight would be stronger and why that made her special, but this time, I was smart enough to stay quiet.

Poor Ry. I don't like how worried she looks now.

INTRODUCTION

Sightwitches are not born; we are made.

Welcome to the Sightwitch Sister Convent. After years of mentoring Serving Sisters, I decided to compile all the rules, orders, and requirements that new arrivals must learn, as well as all the questions they most often ask.

To understand what life here will be like, you must first and foremost understand who our Goddess truly is. Her sleeping form beneath the Witchlands is not only the source of all magic but also the reason we exist. She is life; She is death; She is the ultimate creator.

Many cultures have different names for her, but we know her by her true name: Sirmaya.

The Sightwitch order was founded almost fifteen hundred years ago, when the first Sightwitches appeared in the Witchlands.

At that time, there were no other witches save for the Paladins, whose duty it was to protect and maintain peace across the land. While those chosen twelve were born with magic, our Sightwitch magic is a gift gained simply by devoting our lives to the Goddess. Time spent inside the mountain on which we now reside leads to a buildup of Sirmaya's magic, and ultimately the ability to see into the future.

Over time, the Sisters have honed other talents with this unique form of magic. We have learned that a small cut beneath the ear of a corpse allows us to access the memories of the dead. Additionally, we have found that our own memories are thorough and infallible—every detail around us can be seen a single time and never forgotten.

These three types of magic are what we now swear to protect each morning when we recite the Memory Vow, the Vow of Clear Eyes, and the Vow of a Future Dreamed.

--- ✳ ---

Ryber Fortiza
Y18 D153 — 1 day since Tanzi was Summoned

DREAMS

I don't remember my dreams. As usual.

And I already miss Tanzi. It's strange to wake up alone. Strange to write this without hearing her quill scratch nearby. Strange to sit in this cold space with no one asking, "Did you sleep well, Rybie-Ry?"

Oh, it is true she will be back tonight, but her eyes will no longer be the dark brown of most Kritians. They will be silver.

She will be clear-eyed. A true Sightwitch Sister.

It is worse, though, knowing she will no longer be allowed to share a room with me. She will return from the mountain at the dolmen in the Grove, where all newly gifted Sisters arrive, and then she will move two stories above me in the Convent. She will have a new roommate, a new room, a new life.

I cannot help but wonder if our Threadsister bond can survive that.

A week after Tanzi arrived at the Convent, Hilga assigned us sheep duty with Sister Gwen. But Gwen fell asleep, the sheep wandered outside the glamour, and Tanzi and I got horribly, hideously lost while searching for them. Ever since that day of rain, cold, menacing forest, and unruly sheep, we've been best friends.

Please Sirmaya, don't let that change. I cannot take fake kindness from her. The gift of Sight changes everything. It digs a chasm between friends as wide as the mountain. As deep as the scrying pool from which the spirit swifts fly.

And it happens every time. First there was Sister Margrette, then Sister Ute, then Lachmi, then Oriya. Fazimeh, Yenna, Birgit, Gaellan. They were all my friends; now I hardly speak to them.

No doubt there are even more lost friends who I'm forgetting since I do not have the gift of Clear Eyes. Once seen, often forgotten. Once heard, usually lost.

MEMORIES

I wish I'd been the one Summoned instead of Tanzi.

I hate myself for that.

And just as I predicted, I was charged with clearing the mountain paths today. Summer has fully awakened in the forest that hugs the slope. The weak, fighting buds of spring that I saw last are now full leaves. Green, green everywhere.

On a *normal* day, it would have made me feel better to be outside instead of cooped up in the kitchen. And on a normal day, Tanzi and I would have played the game we always played when no one is around to hear us.

"What happens inside the mountain?" I would ask. Then she'd chime back, "What happens during the Summoning?" For hours we would make guess after guess, each more absurd than the last.

I tried to play alone. To pretend today was no different from any other. To imagine what Tanzi might be doing right now. Yet it was a battle to come up with any clever answers—something as silly as what she might conjure. I gave up after only one try.

"Maybe Sirmaya is not even real," I mumbled, my arms full of fallen pinecones and branches. "Maybe we inhale too much bat droppings in the air, and it turns our eyes to silver."

The words tasted of ash. Especially because part of me wished they could be true. No sleeping Goddess. Just bat droppings and a spirit swift's random choice.

On my hike back to the Convent, I found the two newest Serving Sisters picking flowers off the path.

I yelled at them. It wasn't nice of me, and shame burns in my chest as I write this.

"Rule 15!" I hollered as they dashed for the trail. "Never leave the marked path!"

They tried to apologize the entire trek home, but I wouldn't listen and I wouldn't stop frowning.

I bet they're terrified of me now.

Why do I always do that?

Ryber Fortiza

Y18 D154 — 2 days since Tanzi was Summoned

DREAMS

No dreams. No sleep.

Tanzi has not returned.

Hilga acts as if there is nothing to be alarmed about, but there is. There is. After a Summoning, a Sister returns on the eve of the following day. Almost always, she comes back.

But I waited in the Grove for her all night, and she never returned. I sat beside the dolmen, within view of the slab that will slide back once she has completed her Summoning.

Not once did the granite budge. Even Sister Ute and Sister Birgit, who sat gossiping beside the alders, grew alarmed by sunrise. Then Ute went off to find Hilga.

Soon after, the Head Sister joined us, her expression grim—though she tried to act relaxed, regularly slumping her shoulders and breathing deep.

I know her too well, though. I may not have the Sight, but Hilga was my mentoring Sister for the first six years I was here. Right up until she was named head of the Convent and then creaking old Sister Rose became my mentor instead.

Hilga was scared.

The four of us waited until the sun had fully risen.

Tanzi never came.

So of course, I did not sleep and did not dream.

Where is Tanzi? What if she's hurt? And all alone with no one to help her? There is no way for a non-Summoned Sister to get inside the mountain, so I cannot find her. *No one* can find her.

Curse me. I must go to the observatory now. It is time for morning prayers.

Please, Sirmaya, please. Show us where Tanzi is in the scrying pool. Or better yet, Summon me.

I beg you to. Please, *I beg you.*

MEMORIES

Trina and Gaellan were summoned after the prayers today. No visions of Tanzi in the pool; just more spirit swifts.

Two of them came for two Serving Sisters.

I don't understand.

Ryber Fortiza
Y18 D155 — 3 days since Tanzi was Summoned

DREAMS

No dreams and no sleep.

Tanzi still hasn't returned. Nor Trina, nor Gaellan.

MEMORIES

Three more Serving Sisters were Summoned today.

What is happening? Why is Hilga acting so calm?

And why why why has no one come back from the mountain?

All Sisters enter the mountain two times in their lives. First, to receive the Goddess's gift of Sight.

Second, for sleeping.

Sightwitches do not die. Instead, when our bodies fail us, we enter the mountain and Sirmaya enfolds us into her embrace. We sleep for all eternity, and the magic she gave us returns to her.

None of us knows precisely how that happens, since Sisters who sleep are hardly going to return and explain it all. Yet we *do* know it happens to each and every one of us.

Tanzi can't be sleeping, though. Nor can the other Summoned Sisters. The spirit swifts don't appear for that, and we sleep only when our bodies can no longer continue.

So again: What is happening? I want to know where Tanzi is. I want to know that she's all right.

Sirmaya, I will give *anything* for my Threadsister's safe return. Please, please, please.

―――― ✳ ――――

Tanzi Lamanaya
Y16 D89

Ry and I cornered Hilga after the midday meal today. We went to her office in the top of the tower, where no one could hear.

Where *Sister Rose* couldn't hear.

"Please," Ryber began before Hilga had even reached her chair. "Please be our mentor again. We know you have duties as Head Sister, but Rose is . . . she isn't . . ."

"She isn't very good," I said bluntly—exactly like Ry told me not to do. "She's *ancient*, and she—"

"She is the oldest Sister here," Hilga snapped, dropping emphatically onto her stiff-backed chair. She was wearing her Stern Head Sister face. "Rose has more knowledge and experience than anyone else. You should be grateful she was willing to take over after me."

"But we want to learn more," Ry pleaded.

This was a half lie since I had no interest in learning more. That was really only Ryber. But I *was* dreadfully sick of Rose.

She means well. Sleeper knows she does, but her Sight overpowers her most days—a common ailment for older Sisters and one of the reasons Sisters remain at the Convent their whole lives. It is too hard to live in the outside world with the Sight.

These days, it seems too hard for Sister Rose to live in *this* world. She'll forget mid-sentence what she was teaching us, and no matter how much Ry and I try to remind her, it's rare that she'll ever actually circle back to finish a lesson.

Instead she always feeds us the same phrase, "You'll understand once you're Summoned."

It's so thrice-damned frustrating!

But my argument wasn't nearly as compelling as Ry's, so I let my Threadsister do the rest of the talking. She is the better orator, and also the more desperate party. Plus, the Rook was on his perch, and it had been a few weeks since I'd seen him last.

The Rook is my favorite person at the Convent aside from Ry. And no, he isn't technically a person, but he acts like one. I've never seen an animal that understands so much of what we say—much less one who *insists* we get his name right.

It's not Rook, but THE Rook. He'll bite you if you get it wrong.

"He belongs to the Convent," Rose said this very morning when he swooped in during breakfast. "He is as old as the Crypts and will outlive us all."

"How is that even pos-
sible?" Ry had demanded.

"You'll understand
when you're Summoned."

That had been the
last grain of salt to flood
the sea. Ryber grabbed
my wrist, and I knew *it
was time*. Finally, we were
going to beg Sister Hilga
for a new mentor.

After giving the Rook
a few good scratches be-
side his beak (I love the
way he purrs! Even the
kitchen cat doesn't purr
with this much satisfac-
tion), I honed in on the
argument unfolding be-
hind me.

"Surely," Ryber insisted, "not all questions must be answered with 'You'll understand when you're Summoned!' There must be *something* we can learn now. Fazimeh said she learned about the Standing Stones and the glamour spell yesterday. And Oriya said she learned about the Twelve and the origins of magic.

"Tanzi and I are some of the oldest Serving Sisters here, yet we don't know anything about these pieces of Sightwitch lore. We are woefully behind, Hilga. *Please.*"

It was an excellent speech. Not that I was surprised. Ry could convince ice to melt. Still, I had to fight the urge to break into applause.

As if sensing my delight, Ry glanced back at me with one of her sly half smiles.

Her smile widened when Hilga huffed a sigh of defeat.

"I suppose Rose *is* too old to be teaching."

"She *is*," I confirmed, scooting toward the desk.

"And I suppose, at your ages—how old are you now?"

"Fifteen," Ryber declared as I said, "Fourteen."

"Then yes, your educations should be further along." Hilga fixed us both with a wince. "Do you really not know how the glamour spell hides the Convent from the rest of the world? Or how its magic is bound to the Standing Stones?"

"No," we barked in unison.

Her wince deepened. "Then you indeed have much to catch up on. Here." She shoved out of her chair, aiming for the wall of books behind the Rook. He fluttered with annoyance when she shooed him aside to pull not one, not two, but *three* massive tomes off the shelf.

For half a breath, I regretted our decision to come here. MORE WORK was not really what I had wanted.

But then I caught sight of the elation in Ryber's dark eyes. Her fingers were clutched at her heart, a sign she was itching to pluck the books right out of Hilga's hands.

"Read these," Hilga ordered, offering the books.

As I'd guessed, Ryber snatched them up. She even gave a little squeal of delight.

"Then," Hilga went on, "once you have read them, I want you to come back to me for a list of subjects that you will be researching further in the Crypts."

I tried not to grimace.

I hated the Crypts.

"You will continue to meet with Sister Rose each day, and then once a week with me. Do you understand?"

"Yes," I muttered, wondering how I was going to fit in time for my daily game of ring-ball with Birgit and Yenna. (Birgit has gotten *very* full of herself since she beat me last week. It's intolerable.)

Meanwhile, Ry bounced on her toes. So much excitement! "Thank you, Sister Hilga," she breathed. "Thank you so much!"

Then, as if she feared Hilga would change her mind, she grabbed my wrist and rushed me out of the office.

Now, as I write this, she sits curled up on her side of the bed reading about the Twelve Paladins. Already, she's halfway through the massive book—and already, she's made notes to summarize it all, since she knows I'll never crack open that ancient cover.

THE TWELVE PALADINS & HOW MAGIC
ARRIVED IN THE WITCHLANDS—Notes For Tanzi

Your most favorite Threadsister ever

Debatable.

* Originally the 12 Paladins were the only people with magic
* They had absolute power over the elements they were born to keep in balance

GASP! You wound me, Ry!

Ha. Ha.

* There were 2 Earthwitches, 2 Waterwitches, 2 Airwitches, 2 Firewitches, 2 Aetherwitches, and 2 Voidwitches

Laugh, Ryber! It's funny!

* When a Paladin died, their soul reincarnated into a new body along with all the memories of their past lives
* Sightwitches were the only people aside from the Paladins to possess magic in the Witchlands. But Sightwitches are made, not born.
* Then long ago, half of the Paladins turned on the other half. From "Eridysi's Lament": "Six turned on six and made themselves kings. One turned on five and stole everything."

So how long ago?

* After the betrayal and ultimate death of the Paladins, magic changed. The Origin Wells appeared, and power flowed into all of the Witchlands. Over time, more and more people were born with magic in their blood and the ability to control different facets of the elements.

Don't you ever listen during our lessons?

No

Almost a thousand years ago, lazy bug.

Is that like a lady bug?

 Yes.

---　✳︎　---

Y18 D156 — 4 days since Tanzi was Summoned

MEMORIES

Six more Serving Sisters were Summoned today.
I am the only pall-eyed left.

Y18 D159 — 7 days

MEMORIES

Hilga allowed me to stay after the morning prayers today. I should have been excited. Never have I been allowed to watch as the Sisters pray for a Future Dreamed. Never have I seen the scrying pool come alive with images. All those years growing up when they told me I would soon be watching the pool with them . . . It never came to pass.

But I wasn't excited to watch today. My heart thumped painfully against my ribs, and sweat beaded along my brow.

I was hot. So cursed hot.

What if the pool showed a vision of Tanzi? What if I saw her hurt . . . or worse?

I sat on the high ledge, where the telescope rests. It was the only place I could see into the pool, for all the Sisters had clustered tightly around it. They formed a spiral, Sister Rose at the fore, right on the rim of the pool, and then hand in hand, moving from oldest to youngest, the Sisters spiraled outward.

I had just crouched upon the ledge, my blood roaring in my ears, when the praying began.

I expected a silent prayer, yet I had *not* expected for it to feel so . . . so BIG. Somehow the air in the observatory grew thicker and thicker, heavier and heavier, expanding in time to words I could not hear. It was as if by thinking in unison, each woman's breath and posture and soul latched on to a similar cadence.

All while the heat kicked higher.

Show us something, I begged. *Show me Tanzi.* Though I feared seeing my Threadsister, I feared even more that I would see nothing at all.

Finally, when it felt as if the room could grow no hotter, no heavier, it happened. An image formed in the scrying pool.

It was the Rook, sitting on his perch in Hilga's office. He groomed and fluffed and occasionally clacked his beak.

That was it. Nothing more. For a minute, or perhaps longer, it was just that thrice-damned bird. There was truly nothing I could have cared less about. What did it matter if he hopped off his oak knob and flew out the open window? *Where was Tanzi?*

Yet despite my rage at the vision, I found myself unable to look away.

I couldn't breathe either, and my heart boomed in my ears. The Rook flew ever higher. Now he winged over a pine forest. Now he dove low.

The creature himself swooped into the observatory, landing mere paces from me.

He surprised me so badly, I barely swallowed my yelp, and when I glanced back at the pool, the vision had shimmered away.

Cursed bird.

I hate him.

Y18 D161 — 9 days

MEMORIES

Fourteen Sightwitch Sisters were Summoned today.

This is impossible. Sightwitch Sisters reenter the mountain only for sleeping—and they aren't called by the swifts then. They know from their dreams that it is time to reunite with the Sleeper.

Each Sister the spirit swifts approached today looked shocked. Frightened, even. Yet no one dared disobey the Goddess. If She Summons, we go.

Hilga is worried. Finally, her cool demeanor has cracked. She chews at her fingernails and snaps at anyone who crosses her.

At least this is what she does when I see her, which is rare. She shows her face only at mealtime, if even then. Every waking hour she spends in the Crypts, and each day she enlists more Sightwitch Sisters to help. But not me.

Never me, for I do not have the Sight and I am of no use to anyone.

I have tried to enter the Crypts. Four times now, but no one will go with me—and I cannot defy the Order of Two. Only the Rook will join me. He follows me everywhere I go lately.

Cursed bird.

Tanzi always loved him, but I find him a squawking nuisance.

Y18 D165 — 13 days

Seventeen more Sisters were Summoned.

I feel ill. I do not sleep. No one does.

The mountain shakes, a bare ripple most of the time, yet thrice now we have had full tremors that knocked books off shelves and branches from the trees. Storms have struck too, so I spend every day cleaning debris off the trails. I have never been so focused, so intent on my chores.

I am the model Serving Sister, adhering more strictly than ever to the Rules. I must! I'm the only one left unchosen, and all the Sightwitches are busy looking for answers. Someone must keep forty-four mouths fed and the Convent running.

Today, I cleaned the bridge at the Supplicant's Sorrow, scraping off the algae and bird waste. It took only a few hours, though, so I then moved on to the dolmen in the Grove.

My knuckles are raw. My knees too, and my shoulders burn so sharply I can barely lift them over my head.

What does Sirmaya want from us?

Y18 D167 — 15 days

Twenty more sisters were Summoned.

Y18 D168 — 16 days

Twenty-two more Sisters were Summoned.
Hilga and I are the only ones who remain.

Y18 D171 — 19 days

I know what is coming. Soon, Hilga will be Summoned, and I will be the only Sister left.

I dare not utter these words aloud, though, and Hilga holds her tongue too. In fact, we have exchanged no words in days.

She scarcely looks at me. Her gaze, her mind—they are in another realm. Lost inside the Memory Records she combs from the Crypts. Or perhaps claimed by whatever prayers she offers, unanswered, to the scrying pool.

Y18 D174 — 22 days since Tanzi was Summoned

Hilga was Summoned today.

I knew it would come as surely as if I had the Sight.

It came. It passed.

I am alone.

Two spirit swifts swirled up from the scrying pool to Summon her. They landed on the observatory floor so close to me that my heart surged into my eyeballs.

But no—of course not. Of course they did not come for me. They skipped urgently past and dove straight for Hilga. One even nipped at her gown.

Then Hilga's eyes focused on my face for the first time in weeks. She spoke to me too.

"You do not need to follow me to the mountain, Ryber, nor hum the Chant of Summoning."

It was strange to hear my name on her lips. Strange to hear her voice at all, husky from underuse.

Somehow, I did not collapse to the floor at her words. In fact, my knees had locked so tightly, I barely moved at all.

"Listen to me, Ryber." She reached for the bell-pouch at her hip and untied it in a single, practiced movement. Carefully—frightened even, as if she worried the spirit swifts might disapprove—she approached me.

The birds did indeed disapprove, for one chittered in that shrill, ghostly way of theirs. More sensation inside my skull than true sound.

But Hilga was already to me at that point and offering me the bell. "I have no answers for what is happening beneath the mountain. I do not know why Sirmaya Summons us, and I do not know what the future holds. No clues are hidden in the Crypts, and none of my prayers to the pool have been answered.

"All I can guess is that she needs us for . . . something. And it is our duty to protect her, just as she has protected and provided for us over all these centuries.

"You are alone now, Ryber. The last Sightwitch Sister. This bell must pass to you. Take it."

I took it. My hands did not shake.

Inside, though, I was screaming.

"There are two kinds of Sight," Hilga tried to say, but the swifts cut her off, fluttering their starry wings and hopping toward us.

My lungs closed up; I rocked back a step. Please—was it already time?

Quick as a fighter, Hilga grabbed my wrist and tugged me close.

Then her silver eyes bored into mine. "There are two kinds of Sight, Ryber. The kind that lets you see the future, relive the past, and catalog the world around you in a detail you never knew possible. That is the Sight that I and the other Sisters have.

"But there is another Sight, a simpler Sight—one that is rooted in clarity of purpose. An ability to see the path that matters most and stay firmly gripped upon it.

"I'm sure you can guess which one will serve you better in the long run. Which one will serve us all. Now ring the bell."

I blinked. Then wet my lips, trying to absorb her words. To understand. But they were nonsensical sounds that knocked aimlessly in my skull. *Two kinds of Sight. Gripped upon it. Which one will serve us all.*

The swifts flittered toward us. One clacked its aetherial beak.

"Ring the bell," Hilga repeated, more forcefully now.

I rang the bell.

A stuttering heartbeat passed before the answering toll sounded in the distance.

Then Sister Hilga turned away from me and walked out of the observatory, out of this world, and out of my life entirely.

Tanzi Lamanaya

X17 D254

A man came today. I don't know why, but Hilga let him in—and not just beyond the glamour either, but into the Convent.

I caught a glimpse of him and his two companions when they reached the Supplicant's Sorrow. I had traded cleaning the dolmen for sheep duty today, since out in the meadows, I can pretend I'm far, far away.

The Windswept Plains, perhaps. Or even the savannas of southwest Marstok. *Anywhere* but here.

I'd followed the sheep down to that grassy patch that overlooks the pond. When I saw that we had visitors, I *of course* abandoned the sheep entirely and crept down to the glamour's edge.

The man who led the way—the one who ultimately entered the Convent—was tall, broad of shoulder, fair of hair, and with eyes of stormy blue. At his neck, he wore a gold chain that he fidgeted with constantly.

His companions strode several paces behind. One of the men was just as tall and just as fair, though lean and slouchy. He smiled often and kept muttering things that the final man—a distinctly Marstoki-looking man, who kept his hands defensively high as he walked—chuckled at despite his best efforts not to.

At first, I thought his stance awkward. Then I spotted the triangular Witchmark on the back of his hand.

A Firewitch.

My interest, which had been piqued before, was now tenfold hooked. A hundredfold.

Hilga herself came for the men and bowed to each of them, a sight I've never seen. Hilga *bowing*! Then she led the leader through the glamour and into our home.

So much of the world has forgotten we exist, but some still remember—or still believe enough to go searching.

Like Gran-Mi.

As Sister Rose always says, "History might easily be rewritten, but someone somewhere always remembers what truly happened."

The glamour keeps accidental visitors from wandering beyond. The magic masks us with images of forest expanse and bare mountainside; those who approach too close will abruptly find themselves lost and disoriented. Without really knowing why, they'll turn and walk the other way.

These three men knew what to do, though. They followed the proper protocol, going to the Supplicant's Sorrow and waiting for someone to meet them.

I couldn't help but think of Ryber in that moment. The only child ever to find her way here on her own. To ask to be let in. No wonder the Sisters all thought she would be powerful one day.

I still think she might be too, even if she claims she has given up hope.

I wanted so badly to follow Hilga as she guided the man onto the Convent grounds, but even I won't break a rule where Hilga might see.

As soon as Trina came to relieve me of shepherding, I pelted straight for our bedroom, where I knew I'd find Ryber huddled over a book. When chores end, that's always where she goes first.

Except that when I barged through the door, she *wasn't* hunched over *Tüll's Compendium* or *A Guide to the Constellations*.

She had a child's slate on her lap. The kind with the Nine Star Puzzle embedded into the stone.

At the sight of me, she flung the slate under the covers and then, knowing it was too late—I'd already seen—she dug *herself* under the covers too.

"Any luck?" I asked with forced lightness.

"Of course not," she snarled, words muffled by the blanket.

I scrabbled onto the bed and burrowed under with her. It smelled like chalk, and a streak was smeared across her cheek. "I can tell you the answer, Rybie-Ry."

"No," she spat and, chalk still in hand, she clapped her hands to her ears. "I will figure this blighter out *by myself*, even if it takes me an entire lifetime." Then, as she always declares and has for the past seven years: "Sister Hilga says that it takes some Sisters their whole lives to find the answer."

"Can I at least give you a hint—"

"NO."

With a groan, I kicked the covers off. Ryber gets worse and worse these days about following the Rules, about having to do everything perfectly ALL. THE. TIME.

Yes, I know she thinks that acting like the perfect Serving Sister will draw the spirit swifts from the scrying pool. That it will get her a Summoning from Sirmaya and she will finally earn that powerful Sight like the Sisters always promised her. But I think she's wrong.

It won't make a lick of difference. Sister Gaellan never remembered the Rules, so she constantly broke them by accident. And Sister Lachmi *prided* herself on breaking as many as she could. Yet they're both clear-eyed now, and Ry still isn't.

My poor Threadsister.

I just want her to be happy. To be free.

But she never will be if she won't *think beyond* like I keep telling her.

"Hey," I murmured, poking her in the shoulder. "Why do birds fly south in the winter?" I waited a beat before declaring, "Because it's too far to walk!"

She glared at me.

I sighed. "Laugh, Ry. It's funny, don't you think?"

Then, because I was truly desperate to see her smile, I dragged out the only thing I knew she couldn't refuse: "How about we go swimming under the Convent?"

She shot upright, the slate and puzzle completely forgotten. "Yes, yes, yes!" In a flurry of blankets, she tumbled out of bed and aimed for the door. "Last one there is an earwig!"

By the Twelve, she can move when she wants to.

Ugh, I thought, as I hurried after her. *Why do I do this to myself?* Sleeper knows, I hate earwigs—and I hate swimming under the Convent even more.

Goddess, the things I do to make her smile.

Then again, she does the same for me.

Y18 D180 — 6 days since I became the last Sightwitch Sister

I tried ringing the bell today, to see if it would trick the Goddess into welcoming me into the mountain. I tried first in the observatory after morning prayers . . .

Nothing. No answering toll came from the chapel.

So I tried again at the chapel.

But still, nothing. Instead, the words above the entrance mocked me.

TWO OR MORE AT ALL TIMES,
FOR A LONE SISTER IS LOST.

I am a lone Sister.
I am lost.

A lone sister is lost
A LONE SISTER IS LOST

A lone sister is lost
A lone sister is lost

Y18 D184 — 10 days since I became the last Sightwitch Sister

Why am I here?

Is it because I never solved the Nine Star Puzzle?

Every day I say my morning prayers. Every night I stand vigil in the Grove.

Why am I here? Why am I here? Why am I here?

Part of me thinks I should simply leave the Convent. I do not have the Sight, so unlike the other Sisters, I can survive just fine in the outside world. But . . . where exactly would I go? And what if Tanzi returns in that time?

No. I have to stay. I led myself here by choice when I was four years old. I might not remember that snowy day nor how my aunt chased after me, insisting we continue onward to our new home in Saldonica. But when I found the Sorrow and Sister Hilga came out—when I told them all I was supposed to join—no one argued. My aunt and her family continued on their journey without me, and I became a Serving Sister.

Surely all of that means *something*. Surely the Goddess brought me here for a reason.

This is my home. Tanzi and the Sisters are my family. I cannot . . . I *will not* abandon them.

No. I will wait here and I will continue serving Sirmaya for as long as She needs me.

Lost lost lost lost

LOST
lost *lost*
LOST LOST
LOST

I am lost
I AM LOST

Y18 D195 — 21 days since I became the last Sightwitch Sister

Why am I here?

I have done each Convent chore at least ten times.

I have tended the gardens and the sheep and the chickens every day. I have washed the Supplicant's Sorrow and the dolmen and even the Standing Stones too. The trails are spotless, and the cellar has never been so free of cobwebs. I have cleaned the lookout's nest and reinforced the ladder—something no one has bothered to do in ages.

Every rule I was ever taught, I have followed to perfection. Just as I've always done. I still say my morning prayers to an empty room—though I have finally stopped expecting the spirit swifts to Summon me.

Thirteen years it has taken before I finally gave up hope.

Pathetic.
I am pathetic.

LOST LOST LOST LOST lost lost

Lost Lost Lost LOST lost lost LOST lost lost

Y18 D209 — 35 days since I became the last Sightwitch Sister

Without the Rook here I do not know what I would do.

He is not human, but at least he is sentient. At least he listens and communicates in his own strange bird way.

Or maybe he doesn't. Maybe I'm imagining it all.

WHY AM I HERE?

*A lone sister
is lost*

CHAPTER 3

The Great Mystery of Eridysi's Lament

Many conflicting tales exist surrounding the disappearance of the once famed Sightwitch Sisters, and just as many tales exist proclaiming to know where to find them. Known across the Witchlands for their abilities to both record the memories of the dead as well as foresee events of the future, their mysterious sect has not been seen since the days of Eridysi, almost a millennium past.

While some accounts declare Eridysi the most powerful Sightwitch ever to have lived[1], this humble scholar asserts that she was not, in fact, powerful at all.

I will even go so far as to assert that what set Eridysi apart from other Sightwitches in the scrolls of history is that her final writings are the only ones of which we still have record.

1. See the works of Markus fon Grübe, Kristine Jialla, Raphael Hanssen, or Pitora Abedirashi.

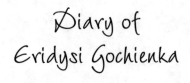

Diary of
Eridysi Gochienka

———— ✳ ————

—— ✳ ——

Eridysi Gochienka
Y2786 D128

MEMORIES—

The first doorway is almost complete.

I am so close. We are so close.

Lady Saria arrived last night, under a veil of moonlight. It took us hours to descend for mere moments of work, yet not once did she complain.

We did not tarry in the mountain's depths. Once she had carved the six doorways inside the cavern, we hurried back to the surface. She had to be back in her court by dawn, or the six Paladins who now called themselves the Exalted Ones might notice something amiss.

What must it be like to control stone? The Sightwitches are gifted with the magic of Sight from Sirmaya, but it is nothing compared to what the Twelve can do. They control all six elements as easily as I summon breath.

I had not seen the Lady work her magic before—only heard tales and read records. 'Tis more incredible than I'd imagined. A single thought, and the granite rippled. I felt it move beneath me, alive. Answering her call.

Though I could not see the Threads of her magic, I could not resist asking her about them on our return to the surface. "How do you manipulate them?"

"I am bound to the earth," she said simply, "and the earth is bound to me."

That was the only answer she gave me—a nonanswer, really, yet I haven't been able to shake the words from my mind. Though we both are nearing thirty years of age, she has the memory of all the Earth Paladins that have come before. Her wisdom permeates all she utters.

Binding Sirmaya's magic to an object is the key to everything I create, yet what I lack is a bond that is *strong enough*.

Not even the Vergedi Knot is enough. Though it is stronger than the Arlenni Loop I used to make my taro cards, it still cannot hold enough power to bind the doorways to an entirely different place in the Witchlands.

For these doorways to open and remain open, I will need more Threads. More of Sirmaya's raw magic.

My head throbs from so much time close to the Goddess. She is so vast. She fills every space in my mind and soul. 'Tis all too easy to lose myself in Her.

And if I lose myself before my time for sleeping, then all my plans will fail. All *our* plans will fail.

The Six and I balance beneath a knife's edge. Which side will cut us, though, is yet to be seen.

Eridysi Gochienka
Y2786 D132

MEMORIES

Head Sister Nadya made me go outside today.

"When was the last time you saw sunlight?" she demanded, having cornered me in my workshop. She scuttled around the room, clucking her tongue at my piles upon piles of notes. And my piles upon piles of rocks.

"What are these even for?" She scooped up a handful of coastal limestone. "They leave dust everywhere, Dysi."

"Don't touch them, Nadya." I rubbed at my temples. By the Sleeper, this headache was getting worse. "Please. Everything is where it is meant to be."

"Except for you." She dropped the stones *clack, clack, clack* atop their brethren and turned sharply toward me. "You do realize that you were supposed to take Sorrow duty three weeks ago."

My forehead wrinkled. "That sounds . . . vaguely . . . Maybe?" My frown shifted to a scowl. "You know I do not have the Sight like you. 'Tis hard to remember."

"Which is why I covered for you, Dysi, though I have a thousand other things to do." Her expression softened. "And I covered the time before that too. *And* the time before that as well. Even though you lack the Sight the rest of us have, that does not excuse you from all Convent duties."

"Sorry," I mumbled, though truth be told, I was not sorry. My inventions and my workshop—this was my world, and right now, I was stuck on this blighted Vergedi Knot. Everything beyond seemed trivial.

"Well," said Nadya, "you can pay me back by going to the Sorrow today."

It took half a beat for those words to settle in my mind. Then I was on my feet in an instant. "I cannot go to the Sorrow!" I opened my arms. "I am right in the middle of this—I think I have figured out the Knot, and if I can do that, we can finally open the doorways. No more Exalted Ones to enslave the people—"

"ENOUGH." Nadya drew herself up to her fullest height. "You make this excuse each and every time, and though 'tis a noble one, I am sick of it. When was the last time you bathed? Your blond hair has turned black with grime. A single day outside of this cave will not affect the Exalted Ones' grip on the land." She thrust a pointed finger at the door. "Besides, a change might shake things loose. Now, go."

I cringed.

"Go, Dysi."

I went, and it was easily the longest ascent I've ever made. Or at least it felt that way. My thighs burned and my lungs ached, and I realized—with some horror—that it had been several days since I'd actually left my workshop in the mountain's heart.

I will say, though, now that I have bathed and sit at the Supplicant's Sorrow to await any visitors to the Convent, Head Sister Nadya was right. It was good to step away. I needed the exercise, I needed the sunshine, and I needed the spring breeze against my cheeks.

The scent of lilac is thick on the air.

LATER

Someone came to the Sorrow today. A man with sadness in his eyes and two daughters he could not raise.

"Their mother . . . died." He struggled to get those words out, speaking in the mountain tongue, though he looked No'Amatsi.

"Can your tribe not help?" I asked. Afternoon fog curled around us, wispy vines to caress the bridge and the island.

"I am amalej." He shifted his weight, and his eyes briefly met mine. The first time since he and his daughters had joined me on the island. "I am a soldier in the Rook King's army," he continued, "and I'm often away. Please, can you not take them?"

Lisbet, a girl of eight, stared at me, unflinching, with huge hazel eyes. I liked the stern set of her jaw; she would fit in well here. The younger girl, Cora, hid behind her father's legs.

"We can take them," I said slowly, choosing my words with care. "But you must tell no one we have done so. The war brings too many orphans to our doors, and we struggle to find space—much less food."

His shoulders relaxed slightly. Relief...and loss too. No man wishes to be parted from his children, especially if they are all he has left of his wife.

Lisbet, to her credit, gave no reaction at all.

The man then twisted to reach for Cora, ready to pull her around. Yet he paused, his hand upon her dark head.

"May I visit them?"

The question was so low I scarcely heard. And though 'tis not allowed anymore—not allowed at all—I found myself reciting the old rules. "Yes. Once a month, you may come. On the day of the full moon."

A thoughtful nod. Even without this grief to shroud him, he seemed the sort of man who spent most of his time inside his own head. "I will return in two weeks," he offered at last.

Then he left.

It hurt me to watch him say good-bye and walk away. To watch Cora weep and Lisbet grit her teeth against tears. He must be near to me in age, yet he has already lost so much.

But this is the will of Sirmaya and the way of the Convent.

After he had gone, I looked down at Lisbet. She held her sister's hand and tried to keep Cora, halfheartedly, from chasing after their father.

"First lesson of the Sightwitches," I said, trying to mimic the authoritative way my mentor had spoken to me almost two decades ago. "There are no coincidences. If you are here, it is because you are meant to be here."

Lisbet's eyes narrowed in thought, an expression almost identical to the one her father had made only minutes before.

"What's a coincidence?" Cora asked, and abruptly she stopped trying to pull away. In fact, she now leaned toward me with curiosity.

"It's when things happen that seem connected," Lisbet answered. It was a much better definition than I could have offered. "Like when you want honey cakes and I also want honey cakes at the same time."

"I always want honey cakes," Cora said softly.

I smiled at that—a real smile, for already I knew these girls would fit in perfectly here. "Well, Cora, I happen to know we are having honey cakes at break this afternoon. And did I not just say, are there no coincidences?"

The records tell me amalej are No'Amatsi whose tribes disbanded upon reaching the Witchlands. They do not follow the old ways from the East, and they are not bound by No'Amatsi laws nor do they even know the language.

I find it strange, then, that the girls' father would use the word "amalej." How did he learn it? Who taught him?

Ah, it matters not. I have work to do, yet for some reason, I cannot shake him from my mind . . .

⁂

Ryber Fortiza

Y18 D212 — 38 days since I became the last
Sightwitch Sister

DREAMS

I dreamed of Tanzi last night. For the first time in all my life, I recall
a dream.

It was not a good one.

Tanzi was trapped behind a wall of water. Screaming. But when I
tried to reach her, she vanished.

MEMORIES

Nubrevnans have arrived in the South. In three of those long, shallow
riverboats they use.

I have spent the entire morning watching them from the telescope.

The Rook told me they were coming. Or rather, during morning
prayers, he swooped and cackled so much from the upper ledge that I
finally snapped, "What, Rook?"

Which of course earned a fresh slew of avian cursing.

"*The Rook*," I corrected the entire time I marched up to the telescope. "*The Rook, the Rook, the Rook*—I'm sorry!"

I was still apologizing when my eye pressed against the looking
glass . . . and immediately, my words died on my tongue.

Boats were scraping ashore. Right on the spot where the river
bends, slowing its rush from the falls.

Soldiers marched onto the craggy beach, as well as women and men not in uniform but clearly as well trained.

They intend to build something. I'm sure of it, for half the crew turned to clearing pines with axes and saws, while the other half unloaded tents and tools from their ships.

Two soldiers came too close to the falls. Close enough for the glamour's magic to roll over them. But the spell did its job, as always, and they both turned away, confused.

LATER

The soldiers have made quick work, and their officer—an enormous man so pale that it's as if all color has been leached out of him—is an Airwitch of some kind. He summons a wind to lift the fallen trees, and I have never seen anything like it.

The Airwitch captain makes people smile often, though he never does. I can't help but wonder why.

I wish I could hear them. I wish I could join them.

Ryber Fortiza

Y18 D215 — 41 days since I became the last Sightwitch Sister

DREAMS

I dreamed of Tanzi again. She was shouting for me from behind the water. "Find me!" she cried. "Please, Ryber, before it is too late!"

Again, I tried to grab her, but as soon as my fingers touched water, pain shot through my hands and into my skull. So fierce, it woke me up.

Now I sit here in bed, sweating and breathing fast while the dawn birds chirrup outside as if nothing is wrong.

MEMORIES

I went to the Crypts for answers. The ghosts are lonely with no one to visit, so they cloyed and choked as soon as I passed through the chapel.

When the Sightwitch Sisters claim the memories of the dead for their Records, some memories tug free. Snippets of soul that don't want to be scrawled down. Wisps of glowing light that twirl and ooze, they flitter for all eternity in the Crypts, waiting to help any Sisters who ask for it. You give them a word and off they careen, searching the endless array of records and volumes and documents for any appearance of that word.

There are so many of them, though, and they get so excited. This is why the Order of Two exists, for even with the Sight, the ghosts can quickly overwhelm the senses.

Leaving a lone sister lost.

But I *have* to understand my dreams, and the best place for answers—the best place in all the Witchlands—is the Crypts.

Besides, the Order isn't an official Rule of the Convent. It's just a guideline.

Look at you, said a voice in the back of my mind as I stood at the threshold from chapel into the Crypts. *Breaking the Order of Two. What wild rebellion will you commit next?*

"Hush," I ordered the voice. It sounded a little too much like Tanzi, and I didn't need this hot wave of guilt building in my belly. Shoving it aside, I strode through the door.

Where the ghosts promptly swarmed. Their cold whispers took root in my mind, growing and pressing down. Slippery, wordless voices. It felt as if I'd dived underwater. My lungs started to cave and my ears to pop.

Thank the Sleeper I like being underwater, though. Diving with cave salamanders has always been fun to me—though Tanzi thinks it miserable. She rarely joined me in the cold pools beneath the Convent.

She rarely went into the Crypts with me either.

Eventually, when the ghosts grew tired of swishing and swiping against me, I was able to suck in a breath. Able to get my bearings.

I stood on the balcony that overlooks the topmost level of the Crypts. Level 1 is like all the levels below it. (Well, at least until Level 5. I've never been below that, so I can only assume they look the same.)

Row upon row of packed stone shelves spanned the roughly hewn cavern. Far, far in the shadows at the other end, a staircase spiraled into the stone and led to a new level, a new balcony.

I picked my way down the ancient steps to Level 1, wishing all the while that my eyes would adjust faster to the dim Firewitched light of the Crypts. Though hundreds of sconces line the walls, most of the spells faded years, perhaps even centuries, ago. Now there is more shadow than light.

And of course, more ghosts than people.

At the foot of the stairs, they awaited my command. I'd never done this by myself before, and it took me a moment to gird myself. To make sure I was ready to follow wherever they led. At last, I puffed up my chest and declared, "Show me all Records on Sightwitch dreams!"

I realized almost instantly, as my words passed from ghost to ghost, rustling outward, that I'd made a mistake.

I had broken Rule 9.

...is holy, for misc... ...d a disregard for rules leads to chaos and conflict. Stay faithful to all Rules of the Convent.

9: THE RULE OF SPECIFICITY
Specificity of language is holy, for in vagueness lies a path to misunderstanding. Be specific in all areas where words are used.

10: THE RULE OF METICULOSITY
M ...ulosi... ...n is holy, for with carelessness

In my defense, I normally excel at using proper, precise language. But dreams were new for me. As was navigating the Crypts alone.

And now it was too late to stop the ghosts from running wild.

Off they went, dragging me with them. They shoved and guided, towed and chanted, "Dreams, dreams, dreams." They swept me from one record to the next. Hide-bound, wood-bound, parchment, cloth—*hundreds* of Memory Records. Any and all that mentioned the word "dreams" they led me to.

I withdrew no tomes from the shelves. I could barely remain standing. The ghosts were a tempest of cold and strength and loneliness.

It was a feeling I knew all too well. I didn't need more of it to scrabble over my skin or grapple down my throat.

Yet there was no escaping that hollow cold, nor breaking out of the ghosts' frantic pull. Until eventually, we reached the end of Level 5, and here, they all stopped at the dark mouth of a doorway that led farther into the mountain. The deeper levels of the Crypts.

Beyond were steps. Beyond were older ghosts. Beyond were dangers that Serving Sisters could not face without the Sight.

Yet beyond, there might also be answers . . .

Panting from all the running, yet also shivering from all the ghosts, I gaped at the shadowy doorway, my feet nailed to the floor.

I wanted to descend. Of course I did. I had been alone for forty-one days, and I wanted Tanzi back. I wanted *all* the Sisters back—especially if my dreams might actually mean something.

You have already broken the Order of Two, said the voice like Tanzi's. *You might as well break Rule 16 and go below Level 5. No one will know you did it, Rybie-Ry.*

"No one except Sirmaya," I muttered.

Sure, but what good has following the Rules done so far? You're stuck up here, and we're all stuck down there. Besides, I still don't think the Rules are even real.

Such a compelling argument from my imaginary Threadsister.

I leaned toward the doorway. The ghosts gusted up. My left foot lifted. The ghosts swirled and nudged. They wanted me to keep going. They wanted me to see what waited beyond—

A shriek crashed through the Crypts behind me.

I reeled about, grabbing for my knife. Someone was with me, someone was coming for me. Danger in the Crypts!

But it was just the Rook, tangled with ghosts. Lots of them. His heat and life must have lured them close, and no matter how hard he flapped his wings, they only clustered tighter.

Curse that bird. He had scared me. So badly I had to stand there for several ragged breaths, hand to my throat as I waited for my pulse to slow.

And curse that bird again because now the ghosts were too addled to be helpful.

I would have to return another time.

Eridysi Gochienka
Y2786 D134

MEMORIES—

Since yesterday, Nadya has been angling for Lisbet and Cora to be my charges. The last three meals, she has placed them directly beside me and murmured things like, "Lisbet reminds me so much of you" and "It is lovely to see how much Cora makes you smile."

Or, more pointedly, "You haven't taken on any new girls in almost two years, Dysi. 'Tis time."

It is tempting. Cora was so sweet at the morning meal today, growing bolder with each hour she is here. And, oh, how infectious her laugh is. Meanwhile, Lisbet is sharp as a Sightwitch key. Question after question she plies at me.

Did I mention their resilience too? I believe I spent my first week at the Convent crying. Yet the girls offered only a few mournful looks after that first bout of tears at the Sorrow. Since then, they have both been chin up and gaze forward.

But I *cannot* take them on. The doors to each kingdom must be finished. Lady Baile and the others are depending on me—whole *nations* are depending on me.

And each day that passes without a solution is one more chance for the Exalted Ones to discover us. To discover me.

Two little girls are a distraction I simply cannot afford.

Yet I also cannot seem to drop the notion.

"What are those?" Lisbet asked when I pulled out my taro cards at the end of midday meal. Around us buzzed the voices of my Sisters, broken up by the clack of wooden spoons against clay bowls.

It is such a habit. Whenever I need to make a decision, my fingers move for my pocket. I withdraw the cards, a question spinning so I can ask Sirmaya directly.

"These are taro cards," I told her. "You know the game?" At her nod, I explained, "I tied Sirmaya's magic to these cards so that I may read the future."

"Is that the Sight?" Cora asked.

For half a tight breath, the old shame swelled. But then it was gone. I had been a Sightless Sightwitch Sister for so long now, the claws of that truth had worn down to nubs. "No," I said. "I don't have visions like they have. I cannot look at something and recall it in perfect detail, and I cannot access the memories of the dead."

"But that is what the Sight is," Lisbet insisted, and I found myself floundering.

How could I explain this to a child? How could I succinctly describe the magic, the spells, and the all-knowing power of the Sleeper? This was not a Sight that I had been given but one that I had chosen to have.

Nadya came to my rescue. "There are signs in the world all around us, girls. Clues to what Sirmaya, our sleeping Goddess, needs us to do. If you know how to look, you can find these hints without the Sight."

"There are no coincidences," Cora asserted, her expression grave. A student reciting her latest lesson.

I couldn't help it. I smiled.

"Precisely," Nadya continued, offering me a smug side eye. "And the cards allow Sister Eridysi to see those portents more easily. Each card has a meaning, and the magic that binds the cards to Sirmaya dictates which card she will draw." Nadya waved to me. "Show them."

So I did.

Three cards I plucked, as is my usual method when a question

The Twins. Lady Fate. The Empress.

plagues. One card for my question; one card for the action I must take; and one card for the future.

"Ah," I breathed as the meaning became instantly clear—and as Nadya clapped her hands, entirely too overjoyed.

"Praise be to Sirmaya," she declared, looking first to Cora, then to Lisbet, and finally to me. "It seems you three have been matched by the Sleeper herself—and as we know, Dysi dearest, there is no changing what is meant to be."

LATER

After I resurfaced from the Crypts, the Rook pecked and pulled at my tunic. A sign he wanted me to follow him.

I feared one of the Nubrevnans had somehow wandered through the glamour . . . Yet at the same time, I also *hoped* one of the Nubrevnans had somehow wandered through the glamour.

Rule 37, the Rule of the Accidental Guest, is very clear, but I would have savored every moment of conversation before I carried it out.

It wasn't until the Rook led me directly to the ladder at the lookout's nest that I realized who had come.

A supplicant. Someone was at the Supplicant's Sorrow.

Never have I climbed that ladder so fast. I was panting by the time I reached the top, and not from exertion. From excitement. From hunger.

A supplicant had come! Perhaps . . . perhaps it was someone I could speak to. Perhaps, even, it was someone who could stay!

Several minutes I waited, staring at the tree line beyond the Sorrow's pond, until at last, a Nomatsi woman and child appeared. They were both pale as the moon, their hair coal black. Huge, teardrop eyes on the girl. Deeper-set eyes on the woman, who walked with resolve, the yellow grass snapping beneath her feet. The girl had to half run, half walk to keep up.

Once they reached the stone bridge, the old woman pointed toward the island. I couldn't hear her, but I could guess she said something akin to what they always say: "Wait on the island beside the fountain. Someone will come for you."

She then knelt and embraced the girl.

I confess, my throat went dry at the sight of it. I hadn't been hugged . . . or touched . . . or spoken to in so long.

Goddess, it had been so long.

Quick. Efficient. The hug was over in a blink before the woman was standing once more and nudging the child onto the bridge.

The girl crossed, her steps cautious but surprisingly unafraid. She carried a small rucksack on her back, presumably filled with some personal belongings. The woman watched her, waiting stiff as a mountain, and I watched her too.

It occurred to me, as the girl took each of her forty-three steps across the bridge (if you have my legs, it takes only thirty-two), that I needed to clean the bridge again. I had scrubbed it fourteen days ago, yet already algae globbed up the south side.

18: THE RULE OF THE SUPPLICANT'S SORROW

The Supplicant's Sorrow must be pristine at all times, for it is the outward face of the Sightwitch Sisters.

But then Tanzi's voice niggled at me again. *Why bother, Ry? There's no one around to see.*

"I am the last Sightwitch Sister," I murmured, "and if I don't follow the Rules, Tanz, then what's the point of being?" Yet even as I said it, I couldn't shake the feeling that there *was* no here in being here.

And I couldn't shake the feeling that I should have gone deeper into the Crypts.

When at last the child reached the island, the woman swiveled away and strode off into the pine trees. Not gone forever, I didn't think. Since supplicants were not always welcomed inside.

Normally, a Sister would scurry out to the island as soon as she'd spotted the supplicant, but sometimes that took hours. The Sorrow was not observed all day; duty in the nest was only a few hours in the afternoon. So oftentimes, supplicants had to wait.

The day slid past.

For almost eight hours, the girl waited on the island for "someone to come for her"—for *me* to come for her. I, in turn, waited to see what she would do.

Yes, so lonely have I become that the prospect of company set my heart to racing with excitement.

I am pathetic.

But by the Sleeper, it was so much like that day nine years ago when Tanzi had been left by her grandmother. It was the first time Hilga let me go with her to the Sorrow, and I had been there to welcome little Tanzi into our ranks.

Not that I was very nice. She still teases me for how stiff I was . . .

Teases? Teased?

Teases. Because of course, Tanzi is still alive, and she'll be back any day now. If I don't find her first.

Yet I could not greet this new child like I had Tanzi. I couldn't welcome her into the Convent.

Never.

I might break the Order of Two—and perhaps even Rule 9—but I only risked myself then. To break Rule 12 about accepting new children . . . That put someone else's life at stake.

Not an option.

Although that truth didn't keep me from imagining what it would be like to go to the girl. A hundred times over the course of the day, I dreamed it out in great detail.

She was clearly such a smart child—and fearless too. First, she explored the narrow spit of the island, even dipping her toes in the pond around it. Then she peered into the fountain, but there's nothing to see. It was drained decades ago, and the carvings of the Twelve that once lined the granite floor have eroded into blank ovals of striated nothing.

The girl dismissed it in a heartbeat and moved to the northern shore where the land slants up into a tiny stone cliff. Rocks rest there, and she quickly set to stacking them. Taller, taller. She spent hours assembling pile after pile, like some miniature architect using strategy and elegance to keep each rock afloat.

I left several times throughout the day. The tomatoes needed picking, and the dill weed had, yet again, overtaken everything.

Yet I never lasted more than an hour at my duties before I would scurry back to the southern forest, my heart pounding as I wondered, *Will she still be there?* Then I'd shimmy up the ladder and into the lookout's nest.

Each time, though, I would find the girl exactly as I had left her, with a few more rock piles towering around her.

Some hovered so high that even with her arms stretched upward, I do not think the girl could have reached the top. I've no idea how she got the stones up there.

Sixteen stacks she built, until the ground was barren. Eventually, she ate an apple from her rucksack. Then she napped amid the stone columns.

By the time the sun set, I had decided to retrieve her. To take her into the Convent, though it would surely be a death sentence for us both.

In fact, I had convinced myself that, *No!* Of course the woman would not return for the girl, and it would be more cruel to leave her here, where she would die of starvation, than to bring her in, where at least we could slowly rot away together.

"Dirdra!"

The voice, a cry from the forest, toppled my desperate daydream and startled the child out of another nap.

"Dirdra!" the woman called again, and this time, she coalesced from the forest's frayed edge.

The girl scrambled up, knocking into one of her piles. Somehow, though, it did not fall. It wobbled and swayed dangerously, yet remained upright. I might have wondered more at that had my heart not been splitting in two as I watched the girl scamper off.

Over the bridge she went, and into the woman's waiting arms. A quick embrace before she shooed the girl into the woods without her. She waited until the girl was out of sight before marching to the island, around the fountain, and finally to the northern shore.

She looked directly at me.

I immediately dropped to my knees.

"Why will you not take her?" she shouted in accented Cartorran. "She is clever and she listens well! Please, Sightwitch, we have nowhere else to leave her."

She can see me, I thought, crawling away from the nest's edge. *She can see me and the glamour has failed and I am exposed.* I half fell down the ladder trying to get away. I needed to check on the Standing Stones—somehow, they must have broken and the glamour had fallen.

SHE COULD SEE ME.

"She will die out here," the woman cried after me. "I am begging you to take her, Sightwitch. Please!"

I paused then, my pulse hammering in my eardrums. If I didn't answer, would she follow? If the glamour was down, there was nothing to keep her outside the Convent grounds.

So I swiveled back and cupped my mouth. "And she will die here too! The Sightwitches are all gone, and there can be no home for her at the Convent."

With that, I spun on my heel and sprinted directly for the Standing Stones.

It is only now, as I sit against the tallest monolith of the eight while the last of the day's light fades, that I realize the woman must have been a Threadwitch.

All the Standing Stones are intact, which means the glamour spell that is bound to them still holds. She must have seen my Threads—not me—through the magic.

Which means she did not hear my answer.

Which means she will never know why I couldn't take in little Dirdra.

For some reason, this makes me cry.

And cry and cry and cry and cry.

The grass tickles my ankles. The Rook preens atop a smaller stone nearby.

I miss Tanzi.

✳

Tanzi Lamanaya

X14 D27

NOTES ON RULE 12: ACCEPTING CHILDREN TO THE CONVENT

Long ago, the Sightwitch Sister Convent was vast place, spanning half the mountain, and the Sisters took in every girl who was ever left at the Sorrow.

"But that was centuries ago," Hilga explained in our meeting today. "In the days of the Twelve, when we Sightwitches were top advisers to queens and kings. When the wealthy and the poor alike sent their corpses here so we could record their memories.

"We had food, we had wealth, and we had space. The Standing Stones had not yet been erected, so no glamour hid us from the world."

"Why was the spell made?" Ry asked. "Why did we hide?"

"Because six Paladins turned on the other six, and we were no longer safe." Hilga lifted a flat-palmed hand before Ryber could inevitably demand more explanation. "That's a lesson for another time. All you need to know now is that the day the spell was cast was the day the Rules of the Convent grew stricter. Including Rule 12.

"So you must harden your hearts, girls, for more children will always be left than we can safely keep. And always, *always* their parents will beg or scream, or curse you when you ignore them. And always, *always* they will say, 'This child will die if you do not take her!'

"But you must not listen, and you must not believe. Look to the Rules to guide you, and remember to trust Sirmaya."

12: THE RULE OF ACCEPTING CHILDREN

1. There must always be at least five Sightwitch Sisters for every one Serving Sister.

2. There must always be more food than sisters, so new children may only be accepted during late fall and winter, when winter reserves are stored and quantities known.

When the sky splits and the mountain quakes,
Make time for good-byes,
For the Sleeper soon breaks.

—**Sightwitch Sister skipping song**

Ryber Fortiza

Y18 D216 — 42 days since I became the last Sightwitch Sister

DREAMS

The same dream came to me, except this time, Hilga was there too. "Find us! Please, Ryber, before it is too late!"`

Two Sisters trapped behind a wall of water.

Two Sisters I could not save.

MEMORIES

I don't know where to start. The day feels so long and disjointed. So much has happened since I wrote my dreams.

So much has *changed*.

But "there is no such thing as coincidence" and "there is no changing what is meant to be." So I must accept this.

"The beginning," Tanzi would say if she were here. "Start your tale at the beginning."

Morning prayers it is, then.

I recited them as I always do, and no spirit swifts came for me. As soon as I'd uttered the final word, I scurried up to the telescope.

The Nubrevnans have made such progress, and their wooden scaffolding looks more and more like a proper tower.

They scuttled about even more industriously today, though their pale-haired captain was nowhere in sight. I couldn't help but wonder where he'd gone.

The storm clouds gathering above the mountains must have spurred the workers on. Black thunderheads were not unusual for this time of year, except that these rolled in from the Northwest.

I've never seen a storm come from Arithuania before.

Eventually my eyes burned from the all the squinting, and lightning had begun to flicker. I needed to check on the sheep, not to mention cover the weaker vegetables and fruits.

Ever the dutiful Serving Sister.

That was when it happened. As I turned away from the telescope and toward the stairs, movement caught my eye.

Movement in the scrying pool.

Nothing unusual. I see flickers atop the water all the time. Ripples of sunlight or the Rook's reflection as he coasts past. I'd already dismissed this particular distraction before my gaze had even locked upon it.

I was wrong, though. For once, it was not sunlight, it was not a reflection.

Shapes were forming on the water. One after the other, elongated figures that grew clearer and larger with each passing boom of my heart. It was as if they walked toward me, people trapped in a rainstorm and reaching for my help.

Before the image had crystallized, I found myself stumbling down the stairs, grasping, clawing for them as desperately as they clawed for me.

Then I was at the pool's rim and falling to my knees as every single Sightwitch Sister stared at me. There was Trina, there was Birgit, there were Gaellan and Ute and Lachmi.

There was Hilga.

There was Tanzi.

Their mouths worked in unison, saying the same phrase again and again. I couldn't hear them, but I didn't need to. I'd heard the words often enough in my dreams.

"Find us," they said. "Please, Ryber, before it is too late!"

"Where?" I cried. My fingers ached to grab at the water; my legs itched to jump in. "Where are you? How do I find you? How, how, how? Please, Tanz," I begged, staring at her. Then at Hilga. "Please, tell me how to find you!"

But the Sisters gave me no answers, and in moments, the entire vision had melted away.

I stared, too scared to exhale. Too scared to do anything that might break this moment and keep a second vision from coming.

Surely another vision would come.

Minutes slid past; no second vision showed.

I touched the water then. I punched my fist into the pool and screamed at the stained-glass ceiling overhead. I screamed at Sirmaya, I screamed at the Sisters, and I screamed at myself.

For never had I felt this truth more sharply than in that moment. A LONE SISTER IS LOST.

Eventually, my throat was too raw to keep shouting. My soul too tired to care. I sank to the stones, curled onto my side, and wept.

Only the storm prompted me to move.

Not the Rook, who tried for an hour to nudge me off the observatory floor. Not my bladder, which had long since moved past discomfort and into misery. Not even my bloodied knees—the result of falling to the stone floor—could wrest me off my spot beside the scrying pool.

The storm, though, was not to be ignored. So bright was the lightning that it seared through my closed eyelids, and so strong was the thunder that it shook through my body with each crash.

This storm was not confined to the sky. The mountain herself was moving.

I pushed myself upright. Stars dotted my vision. Everything hurt. It was in this moment, as the Rook cooed happily that I was finally moving, that a second vision appeared.

Hilga. Alone. Her lips forming new words.

I did not move. I did not breathe. I can't even gauge how long I sat like that, my gaze fixed on her face—on her mouth, silently working with words I could not discern.

Until she wasn't silent anymore.

"Twelve turns," she said, her voice a mere sliver of muted sound. "Twelve turns. Then it will be too late."

Twelve turns. She meant the hourglass in her office. Each flip sent quicksilver dripping down for exactly one hour.

Which meant I had twelve hours until it would be too late to save my Sisters.

Between one heartbeat and the next, I was on my feet, swaying and almost tripping as I bolted for the door.

The Rules of the Convent could be damned. The Sisters needed me to enter the mountain.

Now all I had to do was figure out how.

LATER

I went about my descent with methodical precision. Tanzi could tease me for it all she wanted *after* I found her. But I was not going to enter the mountain un-Summoned without having prepared for every possibility.

True, I still did not know how to enter the mountain, but there was a certainty brewing in my gut. Ever since leaving the observatory, I felt sure. I felt alive. I felt right.

This was the path that was meant for me, and I would not go astray.

Though the storm soaked me through as I raced from one place to the next—from the observatory to the Convent to the Crypts and back to the Convent—I had too much to do to care. Icy rain could not slow me. Wind and falling branches could not deter me.

First things first, I found the hourglass in Hilga's office and flipped it. Quicksilver dripped.

I estimated I'd already lost a quarter of an hour, so I had eleven more flips to get to Tanzi and the others.

I would not waste a moment, but I also would not leave without preparation. The other Sisters might survive a day or two in the mountain, but they had been Summoned.

I was bashing my way in.

With the ghosts' help, I found records on cave exploration in the upper levels of the Crypts. From these, I learned that warm and waterproof layers were key to my survival. I also read records on travel, so I could estimate how much food (and the best types) to pack. I found Sister Rose's healer kit under her cot, and then I used a hammer to chip off a Water-witched purifying stone from the

well. Firewitched matches, a lantern, and a cooking pot—everything went into my quickly expanding satchel.

I even explored the guard room, hoping to find a suitable weapon to bring with me. Yet after finally settling on a saber and then slashing it several times through the air, something Sister Lachmi once said swelled in my mind.

"Never carry a weapon you do not know how to use," I quoted aloud to the Rook, who watched me from atop a suit of armor. "It is more likely to be turned against you than provide any actual defense. Well"—I flung a pointed look at the bird—"I certainly do not know how to use this saber, nor anything else in here. What do you think? Should I go empty-handed?"

The Rook fluffed his feathers in what could only be deemed agreement.

I'd already made up my mind anyway. I had my Sightwitch Sister knife; it would have to be enough.

The last thing I did before forging into the mountain was crawl back up to the telescope and survey the Nubrevnans one last time.

In hindsight, I shouldn't have checked. It was just an excuse to dally, for part of me—a rather large part—hoped that another vision might appear. Something to show exactly *how* to enter the mountain.

But no such vision came, and instead, a scene of chaos and death met my eye through the telescope's lens.

The storm had decimated the Nubrevnans. Their new tower had cracked clean in half, and one of their ships was smashed, while the other two were missing entirely.

"Oh, Sleeper," I whispered, my hands moving to my throat. "Oh, Sleeper, oh, Sleeper."

A cyclone had clearly charged through, and there was no missing the corpses laid in a crooked row upon the riverbank—one of which, I thought, had to be the Airwitch captain, for the man was nowhere in sight.

For some reason, this made me sad.

To make it worse, rain still fell. The soldiers and civilians left behind, the ones forced to reassemble this hell-scape, could not even get a funeral pyre lit. Wet smoke huffed into the air where they tried.

I almost abandoned my course to go help. I had food, I had shelter, I had Firewitched matches that could burn through even the toughest of Sirmaya's storms.

No. The word blasted through my mind, and I rocked back from the telescope. Not only would it break almost every Convent Rule to invite those people behind the glamour, but Tanzi and the Sisters needed me.

"Helping them is not your path right now," I told myself, fists clenching as I walked stiff-backed away from the telescope, off the ledge, and down to the scrying pool, where my satchel and a waxed-canvas cloak awaited me.

By the Twelve, though, it is impossible to watch suffering and not want to extend a hand.

As I shrugged into my cloak and tightened the satchel's straps around my shoulders, my chest, my waist, I recited four words: "Firmly gripped upon it."

Then again as I rang the Summoning bell. "Firmly gripped upon it."

And again when no answering bell tolled.

Each step I took out of the observatory, then squelching up the mountain path to the Crypts, I said those words.

The Rook flew ahead, a patch of black in a world of gray, until at last we reached the chapel.

I stepped inside; the sound of the storm reared back. No more rain to pelt my hooded head.

The Rook followed me inside, where he settled atop a crooked brick over the Crypts door. He watched while I checked one final time that I had everything I needed.

I was ready.

"You can't come with me," I told the Rook as I shook off my sleeves. I was already cold from the rain, and the journey had scarcely begun. "I have no idea what I'll face in the deeper levels, much less once I'm inside the mountain."

Assuming you can get inside the mountain at all, said a voice at the back of my brain. I shoved it aside.

"You need to wait up here, Rook—"

He bristled.

"*The* Rook," I amended hastily, finally glancing his way. He looked decidedly displeased, his beak turned down and his eyes locked on mine. "Someone has to keep an eye on the Convent while I'm gone."

I advanced one step toward the door.

He clacked his beak and opened his wings.

I stepped again, and this time he screeched. A clear threat of, "*I will dive at you if you do not let me join you.*"

"Please, the Rook," I begged, mimicking Tanzi's best pity-me face. "You know how much you hate the ghosts—they'll only be worse in the deeper levels."

That seemed to give him pause. His wings slumped.

"And there won't be any sweets for you to eat either. No jam or honey cakes."

Now he looked mildly appalled.

"Plus, the passages will be so narrow, you probably won't be able to fly. You'll have to hop everywhere!"

Finally, his wings furled entirely and his head sank. But rather than feel triumphant, a prickly sadness unwound in my chest.

I would have liked to have his company. Especially since the words A LONE SISTER IS LOST were carved into a wall mere paces behind me.

I gulped, fists clenching, and whispered, "Firmly gripped upon it."

Then before my courage could falter, I pushed into the Crypts and left the Rook behind.

———— ✳ ————

Y2786 D218

MEMORIES

Cora distracted me today, humming to herself as she always does. We were in my workshop, for I still have much to do and the girls can study their books here as easily as they can in the Convent.

Lisbet sat bowed over a Memory Record, and Cora was practicing her letters, her quill scratching in time to one of the skipping songs I taught her last week.

"One by one into the tombs,
One by one for sleeping."

Yet Cora added a new verse—words that sent chills down my back. When I asked her if she made them up, she simply said, "It is how the song ends. That's what the ghosts told Lisbet." Then off she went, chanting again to herself:

"One by one into the tombs,
One by one for sleeping.
Shadows, fissures, cleft in two,
As one by one comes creeping."

When I asked Lisbet if she truly had heard these new lines from the ghosts, her response only made the chills worsen. "Of course,

Dysi," she said in that serious way of hers. "Don't you hear them saying it too? They certainly want you to hear."

"They want me to hear," I repeated, trying to sort out what her words might mean.

She took it as a question, nodding sharply. "Oh, yes. It's a warning for us all, but no one ever seems to listen."

LATER

I noticed tonight at the evening meal that Lisbet's eyes are clearing.

Yes, already. She has not even been Summoned to the heart of the mountain, but *already* flecks of silver speckle her hazel eyes.

I do not know why this frightens me, and when I draw the cards, they offer me no help.

—— ✳ ——

I was a fool to worry. The lower Crypts were not so different from the higher levels.

Yes, the Firewitched lanterns were fewer and farther between. And yes, the air turned heavier, the weight of the mountain pressing ever harder. The biggest difference, though, was how quickly the temperature plunged.

Level 6, I was comfortable enough. Level 7, less so. By the time I was halfway across Level 8, my teeth were chattering and my breath plumed. I had to huddle deep in my cloak with my hands stuffed into my tunic pockets.

Gloves, I thought. *I should have brought gloves.* I puffed an exhale, and it twined around ghosts that flittered close.

Fewer than I'd guessed. Far fewer. As if the memories here were so old, the ghosts had finally settled back onto the page.

I was especially regretting the absence of gloves when I reached the stairwell down to Level 9. So dark was its snaking tunnel that I had to stop and rummage the lantern from my pack—a Firewitched lantern, for at least in this regard I had come fully prepared. No flint nor flame to worry about. Just a whispered "Ignite."

Then down I went.

When I eventually stepped out of the stairs and onto the balcony of Level 9, I drew up short. Where the ghosts had been silent and absent before, now they rushed at me. A tidal wave of whispers and wind that sent me doubling over.

I couldn't see a thing. Only the fan of yellow light that sprayed out from the lantern at my feet.

The cold, the pressure, the ghosts, and the darkness—this is what death must feel like. Trapped, with chains of ice and whispers to pin you down. I wanted to return to the blessed silence, just for a moment—

"No," I spat. "I am firmly gripped upon it." Though I lacked the Sight, I knew how to follow rules. How to do what needed to be done.

After scooping up the lantern, I set off once more. Ten paces—that was as far as I could see ahead. Enough to descend the steep stairs onto the main floor of Level 9. Enough to set off down the central thoroughfare that bisected the shelves exactly like every other level.

The ghosts followed, clotting thickly. A haze to dampen my lantern's glow. A roar of indecipherable voices and angry memories that somehow turned sharper, louder with each step I pushed forward.

Whatever records were on this floor, they were not happy ones.

Onward I slogged. One foot in front of the next. I lost all concept of time, all concept of space. It was simply me, the ghosts, and the cold.

Until abruptly it wasn't anymore.

Between one row of stone shelves and the next, the ghosts fled. With a shriek that set my skin to crawling, they burst into a spinning wind. It knocked against me. I lost my footing and fell to one knee.

Then they were gone. Just like that. No more ghosts, no more furious memories—only the resounding quake of their final howls to shimmer in the air.

I knew in an instant that this was bad. Whatever could scare away ghosts had to be bad, bad, *bad*.

Gulping in air, I shoved myself to my feet and thrust out the lantern. Left. Right. Nothing but shelves, stone, shadows, and tomes.

"Ryber," trilled a voice behind me. High-pitched and singsong.

I lurched around, light streaking. Pulse keening. But there was nothing.

"Ryber," called a second voice, slightly deeper and from a different direction.

Again, when I twisted toward it, I saw nothing. Only swaying beams of lantern light.

"Ryber," came a third. The highest tone of them all and coasting toward me from behind.

I didn't want to look, but I knew I had to.

I turned. I saw.

Three women glided toward me. Solid. Real. And so very, very wrong. They wore silver tunics, their bare feet peeking out from the bottoms . . .

Feet that did not touch the ground. They hovered. They *flew*.

And where there should have been faces, there was nothing at all. Just black skin, brown skin, and pale skin.

It was their arms and hands, though, that were the most unnatural. Stretched to their feet and with fingers three times as long they ought to be, the women's hands scraped over the stone as they floated toward me.

"Ryber," they harmonized in a minor chord. "You should not have come here, Ryber."

Every muscle in me shook with the need to move. To run. Yet it was as if ropes held me down. I could not look away. I could not turn or move or do anything at all.

"Why did you come here, Ryber?" Closer, closer. "This is not where you belong."

No, I thought, *it isn't.* And with that one thought, my body finally ignited.

I turned. I ran.

The women followed.

Not that I could see them. Forward was all I saw, pack clanking and lantern light bouncing. Shelf after shelf, rough tile after rough tile.

But I heard the women, chanting my name over and over, all while their fingers scratched louder across the floor.

What the blighter were they? And how the *blighter* was I supposed to get away from them?

"Ryber, you don't belong here. Ryber, Ryber, you're not one of us."

Somehow, in the panic that spurred my legs ever faster, I came to the conclusion that if I could just reach Level 10, these creatures would stop their chase. That some barrier would keep these . . . these Death Maidens locked on this floor of infernal ice.

In hindsight, I don't know why I assumed this. Desperation, I suppose. An incentive to keep sprinting toward—a goal to reach.

I hit the stairwell and dove in. Two bounding steps at a time I rounded down. My name skittered after me. My pack banged against the wall, the ceiling, my back. This tunnel was even narrower than the one before. Twice I stumbled. Twice my ankles popped and I had to bounce off the walls to keep upright.

Still they chorused my name. *Still* their fingers clawed across stone.

Then I was there. To the balcony of Level 10.

Out I shoved, and thank the Goddess I did not slow. Not yet, at least.

I charged down to the main floor before I allowed my foolish feet to drag to a stop. Then I rounded back, staring. Praying nothing would appear in the darkened exit from the stairs.

Of course my assumption was wrong, for they were already in the room, staring down at me from atop the balcony.

They cackled. No more harmony. Just giddy, hungry laughter.

And unlike me, they did not need the stairs to descend.

Up they flew. Then over and down.

Never have I spun so fast in my life. Never have I reached such a speed so quickly. I launched from frozen and gasping to a knee-kicking charge, my lantern's beam swinging in all directions. I couldn't see where I was going, and I just had to pray that Level 10 was shaped like every level before it.

It wasn't.

I learned that when I sprinted directly into a wall.

As if that wasn't bad enough, when I veered sharply right, barely preventing a crash into the stone, a crunch sounded.

Then another and another, and before my shaking eyes, rubble punched out of the wall . . . followed by hands.

Human hands that grabbed at me. Two snagged hold, and I barely managed to yank free before two more had latched on.

Oh, how the Death Maidens laughed at that.

"No one wants you here," they trilled. "You simply do not belong."

"*No!*" I shrieked, using all my force to hitch free and fling myself back into a sprint.

But of course, the hands weren't finished with me. Now they burst free from the floor. I had to hop and twist and dart and leap as fingers, fingers *everywhere*, tried to haul me down.

No time for thought, no time for strategy. Just forward. Just away from the Death Maidens still hovering behind.

Their cackles were much, much too near.

Somehow, though, I had chosen the correct side of Lady Fate's knife by turning right at the wall. A jagged maw of a doorway glowed ahead. Fat fronds of foxfire reached out from the rock, giving my Fire-witched lantern a greenish glow—and giving the clawing, reaching hands a rotting sheen.

This time, I did not make the mistake of believing the next level would save me. At least, though, there were no more hands to punch free from the rock. Just walls so close that my shoulders touched and my pack hit the ceiling as I careened faster down.

The cramped space slowed the three monsters. Their singing, "Ryber, Ryber, Ryber," faded slightly as I barreled ever onward.

Level 11. I fell onto the balcony, hands windmilling to keep me upright.

Light. Foxfire. Everywhere it shone, bright enough to burn my eyes. Enough to slow me for half a desperate breath as my vision adjusted.

I almost wish my vision had *never* adjusted. Then I might not have seen the worst of the horrors to come.

As tall as the cavern and propped up like a spider—but with four human arms to hold it high—stood a beast with a head that spun my way. Then kept spinning, bones clicking with each turn. Skull-like, it had black sockets for eyes and a grin that spread wider, wider, wider. All the way around to the back of its head, the smile stretched.

It heaved its massive fleshy body toward me, shockingly nimble. Shockingly fast.

And behind me, the sound of my name bounced closer.

I had no choice: I had to keep moving forward.

Down the stairs I vaulted. My eyes were not on where I stepped but where the Skull-Face ahead was moving. It was fast, but it was also big. If I could stay close to the space between walls and shelves, then it could not reach me.

My plan was a poor one, which I realized the instant I pitched for the right wall.

Hands, hands—the same thrice-damned hands from Level 10 began to break free. Grabbing, ripping, towing me down.

Why, Sirmaya? I wanted to shriek as I cut down a row of shelves. *Why is all of this here?* What were these hands? Or the massive beast now scrabbling toward me, its head spinning and spinning?

No time for answers. Just running. My breath seared. My muscles had gone from tired to numb. Everything moved of its own accord. Distant limbs that kept pumping even as my mind was a useless jumble of terror.

Then I saw it, as I reeled onto the main path and a smell like festering flesh roiled over me—Skull-Face needed a bath—I saw the end of Level 11. It was closer than previous levels, and rather than a darkened doorway in the wall, a chapel waited.

Surrounded by brilliant foxfire, it looked exactly like the chapel at the entrance to the Crypts, now so far behind me.

Yet unlike the chapel outside, this one had a door. Twice as tall as me and with no latch or knob.

Doesn't matter, I decided between one crashing step and the next. I would figure out how to open it when I got there. That was really the only path left to me.

I did not look back, and I did not need to. The sound of the monster's spinning face clicked louder; the stench of death weighed heavier.

And, of course, the chanting call of my name, broken up by syncopated laughter, still followed too near.

The door waved and swam ahead, its edges glowing with a strange blue light. I'd thought that was light from the foxfire, yet the closer I ran, the more I realized it was not a natural light but a magical one.

This door was not going to open without some kind of key.

The bell. That had to be the way in, for there was a small belfry over the chapel, just the like one aboveground.

With my one free hand, I fumbled Hilga's bell from my belt. The earth shook as the fleshy, grinning Skull-Face clambered close.

Its shadow slithered over me before I even had the Summoning bell free.

The Death Maidens simply laughed and laughed and laughed.

Then the bell was unfastened, and without looking back—yet still sprinting as fast as I could—I clanged it.

Once, twice. Hard, hard. A peal that rippled outward until the chapel bell answered, loud enough to drown out all that chased behind. The sound split my brain, and relief erupted in my chest.

If I kept running, I would make it out of here.

Except that the door was not opening. I was almost to it, yet the blue light still glowed and the carved wood had not budged an inch.

I rang the bell harder; the main bell tolled once more.

Still *nothing* happened.

Three paces from the door, I shoved all my strength and terror into my gait. I slammed against the wood.

It didn't move.

Harder I pushed, but to no avail. The bells were not working, and now the monsters had reached me.

I whipped around, back pressed to the door. It was so much worse than I'd feared. Skull-Face leaned down. Its skin writhed as if worms crawled underneath, and its smiling mouth parted to show . . .

Nothing. Nothing at all but darkness.

Slithering beneath the beast's belly were the Death Maidens, their arms raised and claws grasping.

"Ryber, Ryber, Ryber."

I dropped the bell. Knife, knife—at least if I had my knife gripped tight, I might be able to do a some damage to these monsters before I left the world forever.

Right as my fingers gripped the hilt, a sound carved through the chaos: a squawk and the flapping of wings.

The Rook shot down, an arrow aimed for Skull-Face's eyes.

The monster roared, then reared back, one hand leaving the ground to swat at the Rook.

But the bird had already looped aside and now flew for the Maidens—who no longer sang, nor laughed, nor reached for me. Instead, they heaved at the Rook and screamed with voices too high-pitched to fully hear.

I had one breath, maybe two, while the monsters were distracted.

I would not waste this gift.

Whirling about, I grabbed the bell and started clanging once more. Meanwhile, my eyes—my Sight-less, pall-covered eyes—swept over the door. Up, down, side to side. There *had* to be a way to get through.

Skull-Face's hand crashed down to the earth beside me. The world shook and I finally saw what I needed. Just as I'd thought before, this door wasn't going to open without some kind of key.

A key like I currently held: my Sightwitch Sister knife.

In a clumsy thrust of speed, I slid the blade into a thin slot. Blue light flashed and the amber on the hilt flared gold. Then a squeal like metal on metal erupted, and with it came the groan of ancient, unwilling wood.

The door creaked wide; only darkness waited beyond.

I didn't care. I didn't think. I simply sprang forward, shouting for the Rook to come on.

Then I was through, spinning around while the Death Maidens hurled toward me. Skull-Face no longer smiled but only screamed and screamed and screamed.

When there was nothing but a sliver of light shining through the closing door, the Rook darted through. A flap of wings, a gust of familiar must to briefly erase the stench of rot.

Half a beat later, the door rattled shut. Darkness and silence took hold.

I was finally inside the mountain.

NUBREVNAN ROYAL SOIL BOUND & NAVY

Voicewitches

FOR: His Royal Highness Merik Nihar
FROM: First Mate Hanna Sentay

MESSAGE:
We were hit by a storm from the north last night.
The tower collapsed, causing three casualties and
fourteen injuries. Additionally, one of our ships was
destroyed, killing four more. All of our witch officers
are either dead or too injured to assist us in
transporting the wounded back to Lovats.

Send Windwitches, Tidewitches, and healers,
immediately

Please note that Temporary Captain Kullen Ikray is
missing. He left yesterday without explanation, and we
have not seen him since.

This message was recorded by Voicewitch Hermin Layhar in
 Lovats , sent by Voicewitch Ginna Tritza in northern
Nubrevnan border , on the 216 day in the 18th year
since the signing of the Twenty Year Truce.

Y2786 D302

MEMORIES

It has been six months since Lisbet and Cora became my wards, and six times we have gone to the Sorrow to meet their father. We had to bundle up today, for the air was brittle and sharp. Sister Xandra says first snow will come tonight.

He was bundled up as well, his black soldier's tunic layered over wool. Otherwise, he looked as he always did, and he acted as he always did. Except . . . *something* about him was different today.

Or perhaps I am the one who has changed. Certainly I grow weary from the war, from the rebellion.

All I know is that when our eyes met over Lisbet's head today, as he embraced her tight, I felt the winds shift. Like the click when my key opens the workshop door, something moved inside me.

He smiled then—an expression I've never seen him wear. And though it was a sad smile, for grief still weighs heavy and likely always will, it was a smile all the same. One that eased the tired lines creasing around his eyes.

Beautiful eyes. Brown in some lights, bright green in others.

How have I not noticed before?

Then he said, "I have missed you."

I know he spoke to Lisbet at his waist and to Cora, who danced circles around him. Of course he spoke to his girls.

Yet he looked at me as he uttered those words, and fool that I am,

I did not look away.

Instead, I dared to pretend, for half a heartbeat, that the words were meant for me.

Even now, hours later, I cannot forget them.

And I cannot forget his eyes.

LATER—8 hours left to find Tanzi

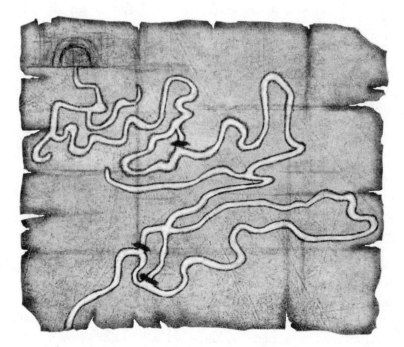

Thank the Sleeper I did not lose my lantern. Without it, I would be lost.

Though fans of luminescent foxfire glow at each intersection, the roughly hewn tunnels beyond are darker than I ever knew possible. Even on a moonless night, there are at least stars to guide you. The Bat, the Hound, the Iris—as reliable as Thread-family. But here, there is nothing. No Firewitched sconces, nor even a basic torch.

It is so quiet I can hear my own heartbeat. I can hear my own *blood,* a rushing sound that pulses and booms. At first I found it un-settling; now I find it a strange sort of comfort. The topsy-turvy world of the mountain might make no sense, but at least my body has not betrayed me.

Yet.

The only other sound is the drip-drip of the hourglass and the Rook's pattering wings whenever he leaves his roost upon my shoulder.

Twice, I have hit cave-ins that block the way and have been forced to turn back. Thrice, the Rook has taken flight off my shoulder to sweep down some blackened hole, only to croak mere moments later in a way that says, "No passage here."

And once, a tremor rattled through the mountain, shaking loose so much dust and scree I was certain the tunnel was collapsing around me.

But it wasn't, and the quake passed in an instant.

I am so grateful the Rook is with me. Without him, I would be lost.

Perhaps I might even be dead.

I don't know.

I have prodded and poked at my memories of the lower Crypts. Illusions—surely they were all illusions. It is the only way that having the Sight might allow one to pass. Seeing and recognizing that some-thing is not really there.

Or maybe it was all real, and those beasts are simply guardians of the Crypts, ready to attack any Sister who does not belong.

When I ask the Rook—in soft whispers, for everything in this place demands quiet, he only purrs and nudges his beak against my face.

WHAT (OR WHO) IS THE ROOK?

A Study by Tanzi Lamanya

The Rook has been resident of the Sightwitch Sister Convent for almost one thousand years, first referenced by Sister Nadya fon Stamfel, whose diary is one of the few stored in the Crypts and not taken with her for sleeping

Dare I ask how you accessed this record? —Hilga

"A nuisance," Nadya describes. "He wants attention all day long and offers nothing in return. At least the cats keep our cellars clear. This creature, who insists we address him as 'the Rook,' spends most of the day sleeping in a patch of sunlight or reading over our shoulders."

Similar accounts appear throughout history, but with little substance regarding what the Rook actually is or why he is here. Ninety-seven Sisters have tried to catalog his diet, behavior, and life cycle, but all studies have yielded limited results.

In an attempt to add to these records, I followed the Rook about his daily activities for three weeks.

And skipped half your chores. You are lucky Ryber covered for you.

DIET

The bulk of the Rook's diet consists of sugary treats handed to him during mealtimes. He will perch at a table's end, beak clicking until someone eventually gives him a bit of her dessert.

Additionally, I watched him break into Sister Rose's cupboard of fruit preserves on four separate occasions. He uses his beak to tap out the lock-spell.

Any diet of actual substance or any diet mimicking that of normal rooks I never observed.

And you did not try to stop him?

BEHAVIOR

Though most rooks are social birds, existing in large groups called clamors, the Rook of the Sightwitches is notably independent. He quickly turns ornery when trapped too long at meals, where all Sisters gather, and has been seen to nip with a certain cat-like annoyance if anyone attempts to cuddle him for more than a minute or two.

As previously recorded, the bulk of the Rook's days are spent sleeping. Though he does give the appearance of reading, often sitting on a Sister's shoulder while she works, I have not been able to confirm that he actually does so.

On the twelfth day of my research, he flew off for three days, leaving the Convent grounds entirely. I do not know how he found us again after that, given the glamour spell, but he clearly did—and frequently does, since he leaves regularly for days and even weeks at a time.

One behavior I have noticed that has not been previously described is how easily the Rook communicates with people. Obviously, he speaks no words, yet the Sisters have no trouble understanding what he wants. My first assumption was that this understanding was a function of the Sight. However, my guess was quickly proved false once I noticed that he has no difficulty conveying his needs to pall-eyed Serving Sisters as well.

I suspect he communicates much as the spirit swifts do, through an intuitive sort of aetherial nudging.

An interesting speculation, but what evidence do you have?

LIFE CYCLE

This aspect of the Rook remains the largest gap in our knowledge, and my three weeks of observation yielded no new answers. At first, I speculated that this bird was perhaps different from the one recorded one thousand years ago, but there are too many similarities, both physical (he is much smaller than standard rooks) and behavioral (such as his diet and communication).

There is no doubt that this bird is indeed the same bird, suggesting he is either able to live hundreds upon hundreds of years, or that perhaps he is immortal.

There are, of course, other creatures known to live forever (or to at least outlive humans by such a span that they seem immortal): sea foxes, mountain bats, flame hawks, and so on. However, unlike those animals, the Rook is the only known specimen of his kind to live longer than fifteen to twenty years.

Forty-nine Memory Records speculate that the Rook was a gift from the Goddess Sirmaya, while twenty-seven speculate the Rook might simply be the result of some magical experiment gone awry. I can find no evidence in the Crypts that either of these answers is true.

In conclusion, the Rook is a creature that, like the Sightwitch Sister Convent, does not fit into the modern Witchlands. Just as we exist hidden from the world as if lost to time, so does the Rook. And just as so much of our order defies all logic—from the Crypts, to the Sight, to Sirmaya Herself—so too does the Rook.

Because you cannot yet access the lower levels. Which again begs the question of how you got Nadya's diary to begin with.

A nicely written sentiment, though it lacks any real substance. You can do better.

LATER — 7 hours left to find Tanzi

The mountain has changed. No more slinking tunnels but a proper passage. Square and with a familiar motif running along the walls at shoulder height.

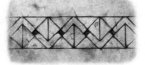

It's the same design sewn along the sleeves of a clear-eyed Sister's silver tunic. It's the same design carved along the fountain of the Supplicant's Sorrow, on the dolmen in the Grove, and around the rim of the scrying pool too.

I've seen it my whole life and read thousands of Memory Records, yet I still don't know what this motif means or where it comes from.

As I walked, I ran my fingers along the grooves etched into the stone, and so preoccupied was I by the sudden structure, the clear marks of humanity, that I didn't notice the gradually growing roar not until I felt it trembling through the rock.

Water. A lot of it.

"Is there a river?" I asked the Rook, and he ruffled his feathers in acknowledgment.

Sure enough, 213 steps later, I reached it. The water's churn masked all other sounds and cut straight across my path, much too violent to cross. And also much too wide.

"Blighter," I muttered, lifting the lantern higher and squinting. Far to my right, a waterfall crashed down, bursting from a hole in the rock tens of paces above.

Behind the waterfall stood the exit. Exactly like the square-shaped hall I'd just abandoned, the path forward continued precisely where I could not go.

For half a breath, defeat settled over me. A sense of hopelessness as icy as the water misting off the river. I had taken the only path forward, and now it seemed to end.

But I gritted my teeth, fingers tightening around the lantern, and cut right. There *had* to be a way across. The Summoned Sisters came this way, didn't they?

Probably.

Maybe.

Either way, it was my only option forward.

"Help me?" I asked the Rook as I swung my lantern left, right, searching and searching.

A huff of air in my ear—undeniably annoyed—and the bird hopped off. In four easy flaps, he crossed the river and glided to a stop beside the exit.

Useless.

"Thanks." I flung him my fiercest glare. Then I stalked back the way I'd come. I fell into a rhythm, moving in time to the constellation skipping song we all learned as children.

Four times, I went up and down the rough riverbank, water sinking deeper into my exposed skin and hair with each pass.

It wasn't until the fifth pass, as I was aiming away from the falls, that I realized I had the right idea—but *the wrong rhyme.*

I wrenched about, light spraying wide, as the words unfolded:

31: THE RULE OF HIDDEN
* TRUTHS*
    Always look behind, for there
the truth unwinds.

It was one of the stranger Rules that Tanzi used as proof in her argument against them. I had always thought it meant I had to stay sharp and aware of my surroundings at all times.

But maybe . . .

In long lopes, I hurried to the waterfall, then craned my neck to glimpse behind. Right there, impossible to see unless you knew where to look, were stepping-stones.

After tying the lantern to my pack and verifying all my tools were still in place on my belt, I sucked in three deep, bracing breaths.

Then I jumped. Water pelted against me, numbing my limbs. Mist clouded my vision, and for a terrifying moment, I thought I'd missed the stone entirely.

But no. There was solid ground beneath me. I was still, somehow, upright.

I had to swipe water from eyes again and again before I could even see the next rock, and I took at least ten more steeling breaths before I felt confident enough to make the leap.

Hop, hop, skip, skip. Four stones in total before I reached the other side.

There, the Rook waited. He paused his preening just long enough to glance at me, an expression of such deep boredom I couldn't resist marching over to him and *shaking*.

Water sprayed.

He hissed and clacked, skittering back. And I laughed—my first laugh in . . .

Goddess. I can't remember the last time I laughed. And it felt so good. A light warmth to fizz in my chest. Even as the Rook catapulted onto my shoulder and nipped at my ear, I couldn't stop giggling.

I had made it.

I had evaded the monster of the Crypts. I had crossed the storm. Now I was moving forward once more.

Just under six and a half hours to go.

LATER — 6 hours left to find Tanzi

My delight over my progress was short-lived. Soaked through from the waterfall, I was all too quickly freezing. All too quickly shivering.

To make my bone-chill worse, ice took hold of the landscape. Hoarfrost at first, a white glaze to coat the stone and mask the wall's design. Then came icicles, spiking down from the ceiling. Some stretched so low I had to stoop and swirl around them. Shortly after that, there was no stone left. Just a slippery, glistening expanse that tinted my lantern's light blue.

I was cold. Colder than I've ever known. My fingers turned to clumsy bricks. I had to stop sketching in my diary. No more drawing each bend and curve in the halls, each rise and step or intrusion of ice. Instead, I marked numbers of steps and turns.

One hour passed, one flipping of my hourglass, yet it felt like days I tromped forward. One stumbling footstep to the next, counting, always counting. Even the Rook on my shoulder and the pack on my back became distant, forgotten things.

The halls were too cramped to risk a fire's smoke, so I tried jogging to stay warm—and to gain speed—but after falling twice and almost twisting my ankle, Sister Rose's voice came scolding through my mind.

"Rule 10, Ryber! Rule 10! What does it say?"

I'd been racing for a seat beside Tanzi in the dining hall. I'd tripped; my bowl of stew had sprayed.

"It's the Rule of Meticulosity," I'd answered while sopping up stew with my tunic.

"Exactly. And it does not merely apply to our work, yes? There is never a reason to rush. Wherever you are trying to go will still be there, even if it takes you longer to reach it."

Sister Rose had been right that day in the Convent. Tanzi would have waited for me no matter how long it took me to fetch my stew.

But would she wait now? *Could* she?

"Doesn't matter," I hissed, toddling back upright while the Rook watched. "If I hurt myself, I'll never reach Tanzi or the other Sisters. Rule 10. Rule 10."

The Rook warbled his agreement before reclaiming his spot on my shoulder. Then, in a rare display of affection, he rubbed his beak on my jaw.

"You're not so bad yourself," I murmured, and off we went once more.

On, on, on. Cold, cold, cold.

Until at last, the hallways changed shape . . . then gave way entirely. I had reached a cavern.

It was like being inside a glacier—I can think of no other way to describe it. Bluish light diffused the space, though where it came from, I could not say. Perhaps Sirmaya Herself, but certainly not the sky. Larger than any floor of the Crypts, the cavern stretched for as far as I could see.

As did black lines. At first, I thought they were cracks. Yet when I stilled my chattering teeth long enough to examine more closely, I found veins of pure darkness wefting through the ice.

I had no inkling what they might be, and I was too cold to much care.

A ledge crooked out from the frozen wall. It did *not* look safe. A single false move, and I would fall straight down to a death of shattered bones and frostbite.

However, right was the only direction to go, so right the Rook and I aimed. We were achingly slow, *too* slow, and the quicksilver taunted me with its ceaseless drip-dripping.

I was helpless to move faster, though. So cold had I become that each planting of my foot felt like someone else's foot. I heard the heel land—and I saw the heel land!—but I certainly didn't feel it.

All I wanted was to stop. To lie down. To sleep.

In the deepest recesses of my mind, I knew this was a sign the cold was killing me. That to slumber would be my end.

Were it not for the Rook pecking my cheek every few minutes, I probably would have given in to Sirmaya's final sleep forever.

The quicksilver was halfway through the hourglass when I saw a platform perhaps forty paces ahead and wide as the observatory. I could stop there. I could build a fire and escape these grasping claws of drowsy death.

Moments blurred past. Drip, drip, drip.

I reached the platform.

Tears sprang to my eyes as I stumbled for the center. Fire. I just wanted a *fire*. The Rook took flight, winging toward a pile of rags against the ice wall. Only with him gone did I realize how much heat he'd been emitting.

My pack fell to the stone with a loud thwack. Dust puffed up, or perhaps frost. I didn't bother to examine it closely because I could not have cared less.

Fire, fire, FIRE. Nothing mattered beyond getting warm.

I heaped out three Firewitched matches, each the length of my forearm. I'd never used them before, but I'd seen Sister Ute do it often enough in the kitchens, singing, "Smack the dough and pound the dough, hammer it and knead it," the whole time.

"Ignite," I whispered.

The magic answered in a flash of light, a crack of sound, and then heat. Blessed, *beautiful* heat to cascade over me.

Slowly, as the quicksilver gathered in my hourglass, I thawed, all while Sister Ute's song tickled against my brain over and over.

Smack the dough and pound the dough,
Hammer it and knead it.

Pies and tarts and bread with jam,
Who wouldn't want to eat it?

On the third sing-through I realized I was rasping the words aloud—and I also noticed the Rook making a fuss behind me.

He clicked and hissed, so with my hands still hovering above the fire's warmth, I glanced back.

And straight into a pair of gray eyes.

A man's eyes.

I screeched. Then almost tipped into the fire. Arms swinging, I stayed upright just long enough to lurch around . . . and *then* hit the floor with a painful thump.

Before me, the pile of rags had unfurled into a very tall, very pale man covered in black oil.

"A fire," the man said in Nubrevnan. "How excellent."

36: THE RULE OF SHARING KEYS
Each Sister has a key unique to her, imbued with the magic of Sirmaya. Keys may not be traded nor shared.

37: THE RULE OF THE ACCIDENTAL GUEST
Should any man discover the Convent accidentally, then his life is forfeit to the judgment of Sirmaya. A woman, however, will be given the choice to remain or depart.

38: THE RULE OF DISPUTED TRUTH
Oftentimes, Memory Records offer different accounts for the same event. As such, all Memory Records are true and all Memory Records are false, for what is life except perception?

A man. Standing in front of me. Filthy skin, pale hair, speaking Nubrevnan.

I would not have been more surprised if Tanzi had suddenly appeared. In fact, that would have been a thousandfold less surprising than this.

My fingers moved for my knife. Poor defense against a man so large—and he was *large*, all shoulders and long limbs—but I would take what I could get.

His hands shot up defensively. Even his palms were dirty. "I won't hurt you. I just want the warmth." His voice was rough as an avalanche. He motioned to my fire. "May I?"

"No," I said flatly. Then I unsheathed my knife and thrust it out.

He sighed. His hands fell, and for several long breaths, we stared each other down. The crack and pop of the Firewitched matches echoed around us. Even the Rook stayed absolutely still, absolutely silent.

The Rules were very clear about what to do with Accidental Guests of the male variety, and I had seen firsthand how that law was carried out. It had happened the year Tanzi arrived. A hunter had lost his way in a blizzard. He'd managed to pass through the glamour, and he'd ended up at the Convent's front gate.

Sister Rose had wielded the knife. No questions asked, no hesitation, no remorse.

"It is the will of Sirmaya," Hilga explained to Tanzi and me later. "And Rule 37 leaves no room for misunderstanding."

But today—right now—I wasn't actually *in* the Convent. I was inside the mountain, and there was plenty of room for misunderstanding.

Drip, drip, drip went the quicksilver. A reminder I did not have time for distractions. For *men*.

I broke our standstill first. "How did you get in here?"

"A good question. One for which I have no good answer."

"Meaning you don't know."

"No clue."

I rubbed at my throat with my free hand. Either my Nubrevnan was bad, or he had a roundabout way of speaking.

Likely both.

"Stop that," I snapped.

"Stop what?" His hands lifted higher.

"Whatever you're doing with your face."

"This is my attempt at a smile. To calm you." He smiled even wider, and I shuddered. The stretching of his lips and crinkling of his eyes made him look like he wanted to eat me.

He sighed. His face and shoulders drooped. "I suppose I've forgotten how to smile along with everything else . . ." He trailed off. Then he flung up a hand, eyes widening. "Um, there's something behind you."

"I'm not stupid."

He gulped. "No doubt that's true, but I'm not lying. A shadow is rising behind you. Very snake-like in shape—and very large."

At that moment, the Rook erupted in a warning of feathers and howling.

So I turned.

I saw.

Ink spilled across the ice. Darkness slithering in two distinct columns, each with a thousand feathery legs on either side.

"Shadow wyrms," I said at the same moment the man said, "Hagfishes."

I flinched. He was right beside me, and this close, there was no ignoring how much he stank.

Of course, my awareness of his stench was a cursory, background thing compared to the approaching wyrms.

I had seen pictures of shadow wyrms in Tüll's *Compendium of Creatures.* Though nothing in that tome had prepared me for their size—easily as long as the Convent—nor for the sound they made.

If it could even be called a sound. It was more a punch of surprise in my chest. Of hunger in my belly.

It was, in all ways, the opposite of the spirit swifts' gentle call. This was visceral. This was hard. This was deadly.

"I think maybe we should run!" the man shouted, voice distorted by the shadow wyrms' cry.

"I agree!" I shouted back, pivoting for the fire. "But not together!" I grabbed for the Firewitched matches. I couldn't leave them behind. They were all I had for warmth. "Douse," I commanded, and the flames snuffed out.

A half breath later, the wyrms stopped screaming. Somehow, the silence was worse. An echo to jitter down my spine and knock inside my organs.

The beasts were coming this way. Crossing over the glacier ceiling, they would soon reach the path behind us.

"I know you specifically said 'not together,'" the man said, "but I don't have a choice. You're running this way, I'm running this way, and if we don't do it at the same time, then one of us is going to die—"

"Enough!" I shrieked. "Come on!"

Another scream knifed over us, but we were running now. No time to dwell, no time to look back.

For the second time that day, I ran for my life.

The wyrms didn't like it. They let loose another cry that hardened in my belly and tangled in my limbs.

I stumbled. My pack listed sharply forward—had it always been this heavy? But the man steadied me with a grip.

"Don't touch me," I snapped, an instinctive reaction. Even with the shared enemy of the shadow wyrms, I still did not know who this man was or what he wanted.

He released me, and the air around us seemed to gust colder.

The wyrms stopped screaming right as my feet slammed off the platform onto the ledge cutting forward. My escape was an overloud gallop, made all the louder by the pack's jangle and clank.

"Maybe . . . they won't . . . hurt us," the man said between gasps. Already he wheezed, and we'd barely begun our escape. "Maybe they're just curious!"

"Curious how we taste," I barked back. "Faster!"

I don't know why I added that command—it wasn't as if he could move any faster. I blocked his way, and the pack slowed me down. Plus, my legs were half the length of his.

Ahead, the walkway cut left, curving with the ice before vanishing around a bend.

Please, Sirmaya, please be a tunnel on the other side—

A thud rattled through the earth. It shook right up to my knees, and a blast of cold seared over me from behind.

"Don't look back!" the man roared.

I looked back.

A mistake, for the shadow wyrms had landed on the ledge, and with the flat, smooth stone beneath them, they were accelerating.

By *a lot.* Shadowy legs tendriled back and forth. Centipedes of pure darkness with no distinguishing features. Simply silhouette and hunger.

Briefly, as my gaze flew forward once more, I met the man's eyes. They bulged and shook, the whites swallowing everything. I could only assume that mine looked the same—

I tripped. My left heel slipped over icy scree. My pack tilted toward the abyss.

This time, though, when the man grabbed the pack and yanked me upright, I did not say a word. I just pumped my legs faster.

I also did not dare look backward again.

We reached an inward curve in the ice, and the outward bend was approaching fast. So were the wyrms, though. Their hundreds of legs kept an endless vibration running through the stone, and with each breath that ripped from my throat, the vibrations shook harder.

"You called them shadow wyrms before!" the man shouted.

I offered no reply because by the Twelve, I did not understand why he was trying to speak. *I* could barely breathe and run at the same time, and he was panting much harder than I.

Yet still he continued: "So this isn't Noden's Hell, then? And those aren't His Hagfishes?"

"No," I huffed.

"That's a relief—"

"*STOP. TALKING.*"

He stopped talking.

We hit the bend. The Rook had already swooped around—I took this as a sign that there was nothing dangerous ahead.

I was wrong.

A third shadow wyrm crawled over the ceiling, just like the one from before, and at its current pace, it would intersect with our one and only escape.

But there was a bit of gold to coat all the chaos: a doorway, almost identical to the one in the Crypts, waited a few hundred paces ahead.

If we could just get there before the wyrms got to us.

The Rook seemed to think the same, and, blessed bird, he gave a vicious screech before flapping right for the shadow wyrm on the ceiling.

A moment later, the wyrm screamed.

And its brethren behind us screamed too.

There it was again—that gut response. The urge to vomit welled hard in my throat, and I had to slow . . . then stop entirely, a hand planted on the wall to keep from losing my balance.

"Your bird is going to get itself killed!" the man said. He latched his hands firmly to my pack to keep me from toppling headfirst over the ledge.

"He knows . . . what he's doing!" I answered between gasps for air, though I wasn't entirely sure if that was true. What had worked in the Crypts might not work here.

I couldn't dwell on it, though, just as I couldn't stay stopped for long. The Rook had bought us a precious few moments with his sweeping and swinging.

I shoved off once more, picking up speed with each step, even as the wyrms' shrieks pierced louder.

If the Rook could just keep that wyrm from crossing the ceiling for a few more moments, then we could reach the doorway.

So long as the ones behind us didn't catch up.

As if on cue, the wyrms' screams broke off and the man called, "Weren't there two wyrms behind us?"

Oh, blighter.

"There was definitely a wyrm behind us," he went on, but I didn't make the mistake of looking back this time. If one wyrm was gone, then maybe that was a good thing.

Besides, the doorway was closing in. I could make out individual planks in the wood, and there at eye level was a slot for my knife.

Fifty paces and we would reach it.

Of course, the ledge on which we raced was also narrowing with each pounding step. Worse, the wyrm on the ceiling now scuttled toward us.

It was right as I groped the knife from its sheath—forty paces, only forty paces—that the earlier shadow wyrm catapulted from the ravine beside me.

All light winked out. In the space between one moment and the next, the world shrank down to me, the wyrm, and the sense of endless free fall.

This close, I could see what the creature truly was: a skeleton of black speckled with embers, as if bones had been dropped into a fire and left to burn. Smoke coiled off it in vast, eternal plumes of frozen darkness.

Then the sense of free fall hitched higher because I actually *was* falling.

Found in only the deepest, darkest places of the Witchlands, shadow wyrms are creatures of the Void. Few have entered their lairs and lived to tell the tale.

Something clamped—hard—onto my shoulders, and my fall ended as suddenly as it began. At first I thought the wyrm had reached me, had bitten.

Then I realized I was dangling, the ice wall at my back and a long, *long* drop before me. At my side, the wyrm still clambered upward.

Cold scored off it in vicious, mind-numbing waves.

I had no time to find out where it aimed before a strained voice called down, "I'm sorry! I know you told me not to touch you, but it was life or death—"

"HAUL ME UP," I screeched. The shadow wyrm had not yet changed its course, but that didn't mean it wouldn't.

"About . . . that," the man panted, blocked from view by my pack, "with your bag and my angle . . . I'm not sure I can." As if to prove the point, he jolted forward.

And I jerked down.

"Sorry," the man called, his voice muffled by a steady boom that now drummed through the ice and stone. "The wyrms are . . . fighting each other . . . and . . . they're tumbling this way."

I had no choice—though fool that I am, I tried to think of some other way. This pack was all I had to sustain me. It was all I had left of the surface. Without it, I was truly on my own.

Another drop downward, and the man's face appeared above the pack. Which meant he was about to fall.

That was it, then. This was my path and I had to stay firmly gripped upon it.

I wriggled free from the pack. One strap, two, and it was off. I had just enough time to watch the bag plummet downward—so, *so* far—before my vision wrenched upward and ice scraped across my back.

Something cracked against my belt before I reached the ledge, where the Nubrevnan helped me to my feet. He was panting, I was panting, but as one, we launched into a sprint—and just in time, for one of the wyrms was angling back toward us, emitting a scream that sent my vision whirling.

I had to keep one hand flat against the ice as I ran, not caring that the cold sliced.

Those screams that were not screams were getting closer, and the stone beneath me trembled.

Twenty paces shrank to ten shrank to five.

I reached the door, and in a frantic movement that sent the button flying off my leather sheath, I had the knife free.

I slammed it into the eye-level hole.

The door creaked wide.

The Nubrevnan grabbed my biceps and threw me inside, right as black cold and knee-shaking screams swallowed all my senses.

Then we were through the door, running—still running—as it thundered shut behind us.

The wyrms had not followed. We were safe.

—— ✳ ——

Y2786 D354

MEMORIES

I met with the Six today, in my workshop and by cover of night. Always by cover of night.

They came to me, each by his or her own magical means. Only the Rook King could not come, but he sent his bird as a proxy. A rook trained as well as any dog. Better, even, for somehow after these meetings, the bird communicates all we discuss to his master.

That rook unsettles me. I wish the King would send his general instead. I've never met the man, but at least he is human.

It has been almost half a year since the Six last met and half a year since I promised them I could make the doorways between kingdoms as well as a way to kill the Exalted Ones once and for all.

But I have no doorways, and I am scarcely any closer to producing a weapon than I was at our last meeting.

I did not tell that to the Six, though. The cards show me again and again that an answer is coming—which means *Sirmaya Herself* is telling me to be patient.

So patient I will be.

"The underground city is almost finished," Bastien said as we went around the table with our various updates. For once, he had removed the mask he always wore, and his scars from the Exalted Ones were plain for us to see.

A not so subtle reminder of why we fought as well as the power we were up against. For as powerful as the six Paladins were that I worked with, the other six, who called themselves the Exalted Ones, were even more so.

"There is currently space for twenty thousand," Bastien continued with a scratch at the brow over his missing eye, "but Saria assures me we can expand."

"We can," Saria inserted. "The wheat and sorghum crops are finally responding to foxfire and magic light."

"And we," Rhian said, "have almost finished the lamps and the heating apparatus."

"All that we lack," finished Midne, looking to Baile, "is a source of energy to keep the billows blowing."

Baile smiled. "It is done. I finished three days ago. The currents inside the plateau will flow and move exactly where we need them."

"Oh, excellent!" cried Midne, and Rhian beamed at her aunt. "That means we can begin moving families as soon as the doorways are prepared."

In perfect synchrony, all gazes swiveled to me. Even the bird's, for of course the doorways are my responsibility. My promise to the Six.

"Soon," I murmured. "'Tis no small amount of magic, and unlike all of you, I was not born with power."

I use this excuse every time—that I am not a Paladin. That I do not have magic. But I know this tale will not keep working forever.

The rest of the meeting we spent lost in discussion. Family by family, we would move the people most oppressed by the Exalted Ones out of danger. They would remain in the underground city to the south until we could kill the corrupted Paladins and end their reincarnations forever.

Although our plans might soon come to fruition, one wrong move could still give us all away. And the violence Bastien had faced at the hands of the Exalted Ones would be nothing compared to the punishment our rebellion would unleash.

When the quicksilver in my hourglass ran out, the Six took their leave. All except Lady Baile. She lingered, pretending to examine my latest assortment of stones. Yet as soon as we were alone, she spoke, "You seem preoccupied today, Dysi."

I cringed. This was exactly what I had feared—that Lisbet and Cora were taking up more of my mind and energy than I had to spare.

"I apologize, my lady." I bobbed my head. "One of my wards is . . . trouble." This wasn't entirely true, of course. Lisbet was not trouble at all, but I did not want to explain how worried she made me lately.

With eyes almost full silver, her mind was in another world.

"Ah." Baile's forehead wrinkled with a frown. She dropped a lime-stone chunk atop its pile. "I admit this was not what I expected you to say. I thought perhaps you had found someone."

"Found . . . someone?"

"Hye. A new man or woman—or perhaps both." She twirled a hand in the air. "It is just that you seem happier than I have seen you in ages."

Nothing could have surprised me more, and Baile seemed to register the shock on my face, for she hastened to add, "Of course you also seem worried, Dysi, but we are all worried these days. What I see in you tonight is a flush on your cheek and a secret smile on your lips. Which is why I cannot help but suspect that you have found someone."

"I . . . no." I could barely swallow the chuckle building in my chest. Me, finding someone. It was truly laughable. "You mean like a Heart-Thread, don't you?"

But Baile wasn't laughing. "Hye, like a Heart-Thread."

This time, I let a snort break free. "Where would I even meet someone, my lady? I spend all my time here, in the workshop, trying to build our doorways."

Baile bounced one shoulder. "Sisters may take lovers, no?"

"Of course," I said, "but I haven't."

She glanced toward the door, where I noticed a masked figure waited in the tunnel outside. "Sometimes we fall in love with those who have been beside us all along."

Ah. So my suspicions regarding those two Paladins were true.

I shook my head. "I am afraid this is not the case for me. No Sisters have suddenly caught my eye, and no one else has entered my life . . ." The rest of my argument faded from my lips, for while I had been speaking, someone's face had indeed come to mind.

Someone who would be at the Supplicant's Sorrow tomorrow. Someone who visited once each month on the full moon.

But of course, I was happy to see him tomorrow—not for *me*, but for Lisbet and Cora. Of course that was why.

A skeptical "hmmm" was all Baile said before she departed.

And a matching "hmmm" was all I could offer in reply.

Y2787 D104

MEMORIES

Lisbet was Summoned today. So, so young.

I am not surprised. She is special.

After two spirit swifts erupted from the scrying pool and landed at Lisbet's feet, she walked to me—not to Nadya—and rolling onto her tiptoes, she whispered, "You should still go."

Then she smiled so wide it hurt my chest to see.

When she returns, her already changing eyes will be silver through and through.

LATER

Cora is ill. Her brow scalds to the touch, and she complains that her throat aches.

"Just a winter cough," Sister Leigh assures me. "I will keep her in the infirmary, and she will be fine in a few days' time."

Please, Blessed Sirmaya, let that be so. Only nine months here, yet Cora and Lisbet have grown more dear to me than I could have ever predicted. "Thread-family," Cora said to me only last week, and I had to lift my hand to hide the tears in my eyes.

Y2787 Ð105

DREAMS

It is the day of the full moon.

I could not sleep all night. Lisbet did not return to the Grove, and though it is not unusual for those with powerful Sight to meet with the Goddess for longer, it worries me all the same.

Cora coughs and coughs. Leigh will not let me in to see her.

Which leaves me alone in my workshop to watch silver time drip past.

He will be at the Sorrow today. In three more hours, the girls' father will arrive, but there will be no daughters to greet him.

"You should still go," Lisbet had said to me.

So I will. 'Tis only polite, after all. Otherwise, he will worry and wonder and wait.

Oh, whom do I fool?

I will go to the Sorrow because despite Vergedi Knots and Arlenni Loops to fill my days, it is his face that fills my dreams.

———— ✳ ————

LATER — 5(I think?) hours left to find Tanzi

Foxfire climbed the walls at all angles in this new space. It lent my dark skin a greenish sheen.

The Rook had already fluttered off down the wide hallway. The man, meanwhile, wheezed beside me.

"Thank . . . Noden," he gasped. I spun toward him, knife slashing high.

It was instinct. My blood still throbbed in my ears from the escape—and from the fall too.

Only pure luck had kept me on the dull side of Lady Fate's blade. How long until that luck ran out?

The man doubled over, coughing and complaining that his lungs didn't seem to work. I gripped the knife hilt ever tighter. I didn't know who he was nor how he had entered the mountain. Fleeing the wyrms together did not suddenly make us allies.

He glanced up at me, eyes watering. "You're"—*cough*—"holding" —*cough*—"it wrong." He waved weakly toward my knife.

I couldn't help it. I glared. "It's still sharp, isn't it?"

"That angle . . . is easy to disarm." Somehow, he looked even more awful than before. Like a cave salamander—one of the slimy ones that Tanzi and I always found in the subterranean streams.

He straightened, wiping at his brow. It spread the black oil farther across his face. "I'm not going to hurt you." He lifted his hands defensively. "I did just save your life, after all."

"I never asked you to."

"Oh." He huffed a ragged laugh. "We can go back out there, then. Try it all again, except this time I *won't* grab you when you fall to your death."

My glare deepened.

"Hmmm." His hands fell. "Clearly humor is not your thing."

I winced. It was too much like what Tanzi always said. *Laugh, Ry! It's funny, don't you think?*

At the thought of Tanzi, I lowered the knife—though I didn't sheathe it.

Instantly, the man's shoulders relaxed. He tried for a grin, though it was easily as terrifying as the one from before. Perhaps even more so, since now he looked like some skeleton-salamander hybrid.

"Sorry again. For the, ah . . ." He wiggled his fingers. "The touching. Earlier."

I grunted. Then, with the briefest of eye contact, I said, "Thank you. For saving my life. Now walk." I motioned in the direction the Rook had gone. It was the only way forward.

The man, to his credit, did exactly that. He turned on his heel, that awful grin still stretched across his face, and marched forward, if a bit haggard in his movements.

I counted twenty-three paces before the hallway ended and a workshop met our eyes, an expansive stone space with balconies and stairwells. Shelves lined the walls, while tables of all shapes and sizes filled the floor, each one littered with papers, books, and a hundred strange contraptions I didn't recognize.

Every available inch of wall was covered in foxfire. Even some of the shelves, leaving the whole room to glow green.

"Noden's breath," the man murmured two paces away. His head tipped back to take it all in.

I couldn't help but do the same. Whatever this place was, it was special.

The Rook squawked from a nearby table. The man and I jumped in unison, which set the Rook to chuckling.

Which in turn set the man to laughing and me to scowling. My annoyance was short-lived, though, for right as the man twisted toward me, lips parted to speak, I spotted blood on his chest.

"You're hurt," I said, and in a moment, without any thought at all, I'd sheathed the knife.

"It's an old wound," he said, glancing down and patting at his stained coat. "I had it when I woke up on the ice . . . Oh, wait. This one's new." He barked a laugh, as if delighted by this discovery, and poked the wound. A great thump of his finger, like he didn't quite believe the slash across his chest was real.

His fingers hit the bloodied line.

A cry of shock and pain split his lips.

Then, before I could lunge forward or do anything at all, his eyes rolled back in his head and he toppled forward. So massive. A tree trunk tumbling over.

He hit the floor with a room-shaking thunk.

I darted over and crouched to one knee at his side. I tried to lift him, to turn him, to smack him awake.

But he was out. Completely unconscious, his skin growing colder by the second.

Now, I feel the need to assert here that under normal circumstances I would have helped him. Even as an Accidental Guest of the male variety, I *would* have stopped to help him had I not seen what I saw next.

What happened was that I knelt beside him, and my hourglass slung down against my knee.

The top half was empty. At some point, the last hour had run out.

Nausea swept over me. I yanked the glass into view—only to face a crooked line of broken glass.

I truly thought I might hurl.

The hourglass was broken. The bottom half had shattered, and the device had drained of quicksilver entirely. Not a single drop was left.

I couldn't breathe. My thoughts sliced left and right, up and down, an incoherent jumble of questions and panic.

I must have smashed it in the chase, was followed by, *That was the crunch I felt against the ice wall.* Then right on that thought's tail, *I have no idea how much time has passed. I have no idea how much time is left.*

I started cursing then. One swear word after the next, they fell from my tongue as I shoved back to my feet.

I wish I could say I'd forgotten the man, but that wouldn't be true. The fact is, I didn't care about how hurt he might be or what healing he might need.

All I could think about was time—that there was not enough of it, that I had to keep going. There had to be an exit from this workshop somewhere. There had to be a way to keep moving forward, no pauses. No looking back.

As I stumbled away from the man, my gaze sweeping over the crowded room around me, Tanzi's face filled my mind.

Her cheeks were bunched up, her eyes lit with mischief. "Laugh, Ry!" she taunted. "It's funny, don't you think?"

⸻ ✳ ⸻

Y2787 D105

MEMORIES

I met him on the bridge to the island, the spring forest at his back and the Sorrow at mine. His chestnut mountain horse, a sturdy beast, grazed near the shore while the morning birds chirruped and chittered in the trees.

Like always, he wore a black silk tunic over a high-necked beige shirt.

And like always, by the time I reached the Sorrow, he was already waiting for me on the bridge. I had come earlier today, hoping to beat him. Hoping to lay out a picnic of the morning's first bread and some of Sister Xandra's precious apricot preserves (I promised her a new cooling stone in exchange for them, though Sleeper knows when I'll have the chance to build it). Yet still, he had arrived first.

As I approached the bridge, I couldn't stop gulping. Or blinking. And my heart knocked against my ribs with such force, I thought surely he could hear it. It did not help that a late spring frost had come last night, so my shallow breaths puffed on each exhale.

Nor did it help that the sun had just risen over the mountains in the East, forcing me to squint to see him. I couldn't gauge if he was happy at the sight of me, or perplexed, annoyed, elated, disappointed.

And Goddess, why were my hands shaking?

I reached him. He bowed in the mountain style: a bobbing of the knees and a hand to tap at his brow. "My lady."

I matched his movement, and then, because I have all the poise of an agitated four-year-old, I thrust out the canvas sack of food and exclaimed, "I brought you breakfast. The girls could not come today. Lisbet has been Summoned, which is the greatest honor and we are all so proud and you should be proud too. Cora is sick, but you need not worry. 'Tis a minor cough and Sister Leigh tells me it will pass in another day. I am so sorry that they are not here, but I hope you will enjoy the bread—"

Oh, Goddess, what was I even saying?

"—It was just baked, and the apricots in the preserves are from this year's harvest. I hope you are not too upset about the girls not being here—"

Stop talking! I shrieked inwardly. *Stop talking, stop talking!*

"—I know they are sad to miss you, but there is always the next full moon. You will come then, won't you?" I clamped my mouth shut. No more words, no more blathering.

Especially since he was not smiling. The serious lines etched upon his brow had deepened, and his eyes—a rich brown with the light at his back—were hooded in confusion. Or irritation. Or perhaps even regret that he had come at all.

"Oh," he murmured eventually, reaching for the food.

His fingers curled around the sack.

Our hands met.

It was the barest touch, his knuckles grazing against my grip. A grip that I wasn't releasing for some inexplicable reason. Just as, for some inexplicable reason, I was staring at his hands.

I had noticed his fingers before. It was hard not to, with such long, fine bones. With such calloused knuckles and small scars to pucker the skin. A soldier's hands. A father's hands.

Never had they made my mouth go quite so dry, though.

He cleared his throat.

I reared back, flushing furiously, and squeaked, "I hope you enjoy the food. Safe travels home." Then I spun on my heel and fled, all thoughts of sharing the picnic long since erased by panic.

Fool, fool, fool—what had that been? Oh, Goddess, save me, what was I *doing*? Hands pressed to my boiling cheeks, I half ran, half skipped to get away from any more heapings of embarrassment. But when I reached the bridge's end and tramped onto the Sorrow's grass, a voice skated over me.

"Stay."

I froze.

"That is," he went on, voice stilted, "I have come a long way. We could . . . share the food? Well, if you have not eaten, that is. And if you have nothing else to do, of course, since I am sure you are a busy woman. I would appreciate the company, though. Your company, I mean."

Now he was the one to ramble on, and as I swiveled toward him, a distant calm settled over me.

He wanted me to stay. Without the girls.

And he was walking toward me, strong step by strong step. He moved like a soldier, yet his gaze was downcast and his free hand kept scrubbing at his dark hair.

Hair, I noticed, that was damp. As if he'd cleaned up in the lake before my arrival.

With that realization, all my fraught nerves slid away. In fact, a confidence began to brew in my veins. A sureness that what I felt—whatever it was—he felt too.

He wanted me to stay. He wanted my company.

So when he strode onto the isle beside me and our gazes met for the second time, I did not look away.

Nor did he.

His eyes were green now, with the light to course into them, and his lips were parted, his chest still.

We stared and stared and stared.

The breeze twirled around us. The birds sang. The horse munched.

I cannot say how long we stayed that way. A man and a woman caught in a sunbeam. All I know is that eventually one of us moved and time resumed its forward beat.

Gone was the awkwardness after that. I had no trouble speaking nor holding his eyes nor enjoying every laugh and sideways smile I earned.

Hours we stayed together, until the sun overhead grew hot in its directness. Until I knew more about him than I'd ever dared ask before. How he was not amalej by choice, but that his tribe had been forcefully disbanded by the Exalted Ones. How the girls' mother had passed away from a wasting disease. How he traveled far and wide, protecting the Rook King's mountain people.

Only when we had to go our separate ways—he to return home, and me to check on Cora—did any of our earlier tension return. Though even that was changed now, our clumsy good-byes fueled by reluctance instead of nerves.

Or at least, so it was for me.

Goddess, I do not know how I will wait twenty-eight days for his next visit.

LATER

I found this in my workshop last night. Lisbet clearly left it for me before her Summoning, but I don't know what to make of it.

Fissures in the ice
always follow the grain.
Unless something stops them,
    something blocks them,
        something forces them to change.

        Then the fissures in the ice
            will find new ways to travel.

There are no coincidences.

                Except when there are.

———— ✳ ————

5(?) hours to find Tanzi

On and on, Tanzi's memory teased me. "Laugh, Ry!" she insisted while I searched the nearest floor for some kind of exit. "It's funny, don't you think?"

Then, as I moved upstairs, her voice sang in time to my steps on the winding, creaking wood.

Laugh. Ry. It's. Fun. Ry. Don't. You. Think.

I hit the upstairs, a wooden loft that spanned into a larger floor of stone. More shelves, more tables, more books and papers and gadgets.

Even the brief earthquake that shivered through the workshop, ending almost as quickly as it began, seemed to move in time to Tanzi's mocking words.

"I don't think it's funny," I muttered. "It's not at funny at all . . ." I trailed off, my eyes landing on another door with an eye-level keyhole.

I set off for it, a fresh surge of strength in my step.

This wasn't funny, and I wouldn't laugh. Instead, I would find Tanzi, I would find the Sisters, and I wouldn't delay another moment—

A storm of black kicked into my path. Feathers and must and a wild clacking of beak.

The Rook was not happy.

He pecked and squawked at me. He flew in my face, and no amount of swinging my hands or yelling at him made a difference.

He simply would not let me go.

When his beak chomped down on my nose, I finally gave up.

"What?" I howled, reeling back two steps. "What is wrong?"

I shouldn't have spoken, because he launched himself at me. This time, I was smart enough to fling up my hands, but he simply bit my forearms instead. Hard enough to draw blood.

I had no choice but to back away. Then finally turn and simply run.

I thought he'd lost his mind. I thought he'd turned on me or been possessed by a ghost or *something*, and now he was going to kill me.

So I scurried back the way I'd come, back downstairs, back toward the Nubrevnan.

Upon reaching the unconscious man, the Rook abruptly stopped his attack. He landed on a table behind me, his wings stretched wide as if to block my way.

Heart drumming in my chest, I sucked in air and gawped at him. "What," I snapped, "was that for?"

One of his wings dropped, as if . . .

As if he *pointed* to the Nubrevnan.

I glanced down. Blood had trickled out sideways around the man, following a gap in the stone tiles and framing his left side.

That couldn't be healthy. Nor could the way his back scarcely moved when he inhaled.

"No," I moaned. I didn't have time for this. The Sisters needed me.

My fist moved to my heart, and seconds skated past. I could heal a man I didn't know and potentially lose my Sisters, or I could go after them and he could potentially die.

Help the man. Help my Sisters.

Except I realized the debate was pointless. When I had lost my pack, I had lost my healer kit too.

"I'm sorry, the Rook," I said at last. "I can't do anything for him, and the Sisters need me. They need us."

The Rook did not look impressed, and my ire only fanned hotter.

I puffed out my chest. "If I help him, I risk losing Tanzi. Is that what you want?"

A purring of affirmation.

"But I have no healer kit! There's nothing I can do here!"

He wafted his wings until a breeze wisped over me—and a page flipped off the nearest table.

It landed at my feet, a torn-out sheet from some book on Thread-witches. Written in the margins were numbers with items scribbled beside them.

The numbers were bookcases and shelves, I realized. Then I put it all together: this was an inventory of sorts. A crude, disorganized one, but the system covered almost every paper that my eyes scraped over.

If there were rocks, jewels, drinks, and weapons in here, perhaps there were other things too.

In a single movement, I snatched up the page and fixed my hardest frown on the Rook. "You're telling me there's a healer kit somewhere in this place?"

Another purr, and this time, his wings lowered half an inch.

I gulped and glanced at the paper now clenched in my fist. I'd broken the hourglass with likely half of the quicksilver in the top. Surely no more than another half hour had passed since then.

Surely, surely I could save this man's life *and* save Tanzi's too.

It was, if nothing else, my only option. The Rook would never let me leave otherwise.

So with a prayer to Sirmaya—a frantic plea, really, that she keep my Thread-family safe—I smacked the paper on a table and set off to find a healer kit.

Anett det Vergedi
Understanding Threads

Floor 2, Case 3, shelf 2 — rubies, sapphires, emeralds

Floor 1, Case 18 — Pine Cones

No one contests that Threads exist, yet people live by them and fear them alike. Terms like "Thread-brother" or "Heart-Thread" are found in all languages of the Witchlands, and were used long before the No'Amatsi people reached this continent.

Shelves 3-5 — quartz

Floor 3, Case 4 — limestone samples

Floor 2, Case 8 — Scorched Land earth samples

Threadwitches, however, did not appear in the Witchlands until the No'Amatsis' arrival, and at that time, a Threadwitch's ability to bind magic to stones was a learned skill—not an inborn power. On the Fareastern continent from which the No'Amastis originally hailed, magic was not exclusive to the Twelve Paladins (as it was in the Witchlands), and such power could be accessed by anyone with sufficient training.

Nomatsis

Floor 1, Case 11 — moths & butterflies

It was the unique ability of Threadwitches to create magic stones that led to the first hints of mistrust between native Witchlanders and the No'Amatsi tribes. Though ethnic and racial tensions have always existed in the Witchlands, such clashes worsened when the Paladins' reign ended and magic spread through the continent. It was also at this time that Threadwitchery changed into the form we know and use today and that the No'matsis' were fully ostracized from society.

That newer power combined with the old ways from the Fareast has led to a rich tapestry of methodologies. Dating back to the earliest Threadstone master, Valya det Arlenni, we begin with the simplest method of fastening Threads to stones: the Arlenni Loop.

5(?) hours left to find Tanzi—

I wish I had more time. The workshop begged to be explored, with its three floors and running water—*not* Waterwitched, but with actual pumps and a spigot.

It was an absolute marvel of inventions. Some magical, some mechanical. Some theoretical and scrawled upon paper. Some assembled and ready to be used.

No dust coated the surfaces, no cobwebs clustered in the corners, and no moths had left holes behind. It meant a preservation spell rested over this space, like the ones that protected the records in the Crypts.

It also meant this place was old.

Old old. Judging by the spellings and grammar on each loose page, I would guess at least a thousand years old.

But there was no time to dawdle. No time to explore.

I found what I needed on the third floor. Not that I would have recognized it without the Rook to help.

A shrill caw as I stepped off the stairs, then he arrowed over to a rolled red leather pouch. It hung on a hook above a spigot (the fourth I'd seen thus far). A quick peek inside showed salves, creams, tinctures with familiar names, and even a handful of tinder with a strip of flint.

Another clever invention, for a small diagram sewn on an inside pocket showed how to start a fire by striking the flint against the pouch's metal clasp.

Whoever had crafted this place, she—or they—had been a true genius.

I didn't bother to roll up the kit before I rushed back down the spiraling flights of stairs and over to the Nubrevnan's side.

He still lay flat on his stomach, his face crooked awkwardly to one side. Goddess, he was massive, and there would be no avoiding his blood while I flipped him over.

Yet he *had* to be flipped over. It took three tries and a full, groaning shout to manage it. Once on his back, though—once I was mere inches away and able to see beneath the grime that coated his skin and uniform—it hit me: I knew this young man.

He was the officer from the Nubrevnan camp. The one I'd watched bellowing orders and building a watchtower.

Perhaps it was the black oil that coated him, or perhaps it was simply the lack of a glass lens and distance to distort him, but either way, he looked different this close. For one, he was younger than I'd thought from afar. My age or near to it.

Plus, the bones that made up his gangly limbs were surprisingly slender, surprisingly soft. Elegant, even, like the marble statues stowed away in the Convent cellar.

Although marble didn't bleed, this man most assuredly did. One of the shadow wyrms had slashed him from right shoulder to left hip, and though the clothing had sliced neatly, the skin had not. The edges were frayed and puckered, as if burned.

Or as if frozen.

He was lucky, actually, for the wyrm's intense cold had cauterized most of the wound. Only the topmost quarter hung open and oozed.

I gulped, then turned briefly away. While I'd gone through the same healing classes as every other Serving Sister, I'd never been adept at them—and I'd never grown comfortable with the sight of blood.

On top of that, I'd never *ever* worked on a man before.

I huffed an exhale. "Firmly gripped upon it," I whispered. Then I turned to the healer kit and got to work.

The minutes slid past, and without my hourglass to drip-drip, I had no concept of how many. I lost myself in the focus, and I swear by the Sleeper that I did not rush.

Yes, I wanted to save my Sisters, but the Rook had been right: I could not leave another human to die.

The bird watched from a nearby shelf as I washed water across the man's wound. The oil—an almost tar-like substance—cleaned right off to reveal skin somehow even paler than the man's face. Next, I rubbed in a Waterwitch healer cream to ward off corruption and followed with an Earthwitch salve to seal the wound and heal the skin.

Such a massive man, all thick shoulders and wiry muscle, required almost the entire tubs of cream and salve.

And finally, because I did not think it would hurt, I squeezed a few droplets of something called Cure-All directly atop the gash.

Already, the man's breath came more evenly. Already, the sheen of sweat had left his face, replaced by something that could *almost* be called warmth.

As I returned the Cure-All to its pocket, I felt something else inside. Paper, waxed and folded. I slid it out—

"You're certain this isn't Hell?"

I snapped up my gaze, heart skittering, and met the man's hooded, glassy eyes.

"You're . . . alive," I offered eloquently. Then I looked away once more.

He was close; I didn't like it.

"Thanks to you." With a grunt, he pushed himself upright.

Which brought him even closer.

"Are there any Airwitched smelling herbs?" He patted his chest—not where the cut was this time. "My lungs feel . . . weak."

"No," I answered, leaning away and towing the healer kit with me. "Also, you stink. Whatever you're covered in, it's disgusting."

He nodded. "Stinky, but at least healing! Aside from my lungs, I feel better than I have since . . . since I woke up inside a glacier with no clue how or why." A smile quirked on his lips.

It was much less scary than his previous grins.

"What's your name?" he asked, eyebrows bouncing. He really did look a thousand times better than he had only minutes before.

That Cure-All must be special stuff.

"Ryber Fortiza," I answered before I could think better of it.

"Ryberta Fortsa," he murmured to himself. "Very Nubrevnan."

"It is not!" I smacked the pouch shut for emphasis—or tried to, but the paper inside got caught. Forcing me to yank it out and try again. "Because that is not my name!"

He had the grace to flush.

"My name is Illryan," I went on. "It's RY. BER—no 'ta' on the end—and then FOR. TEE. ZAH. Not . . . whatever it is you just said."

"Ry-ber," he repeated, smiling once more. "For-tee-zah. Understood."

"Hmph," was all I replied as I finished fastening the pouch and stood. The room listed; my stomach growled.

There was nothing to be done for hunger, though. Preserving books and inventions was one thing. Food was quite another.

"Careful now," the young man said, reaching for me.

I recoiled. "I'm fine."

He winced, hand withdrawing. "Sorry. No touching. I should

know better by now." He tried for one of his smiles, but this one was strained.

"I don't know *your* name," I said, an attempt to change the subject.

"Something we have in common, then," he replied. "I don't know what my name is either."

I blinked. "No idea . . . at all?"

"No idea at all."

"I think I saw you," I began, scooping up the healer pouch and folded paper. "You're an officer in the Nubrevnan navy, and you were building a watchtower."

"Perhaps." He glanced down at his wound, the first time he'd shown any interest in it since waking. His forehead bunched tight, and I don't think I imagined that the room turned suddenly colder.

Then I remembered. "You're an Airwitch too."

"Oh, right." He lifted his left hand, where sure enough, mingled amid the oil was a diamond tattoo. "I saw that earlier, but if I have magic, I can't seem to find it."

"I don't think that's how witcheries work." I stepped toward him, already planning all the ways we could use his magic to navigate the rest of the mountain. "A little time, and I'm sure you'll be able to use it again."

The Rook piped up then, crowing his agreement. Not that the man understood. He just nodded at the bird. "A pleasure to meet you too. And your name is . . . ?"

"He's the Rook," I answered.

"Very nice." The young man saluted, fist to his heart.

The Rook liked this, for he instantly flapped over to the man's side and started purring.

Traitor. He knew I wanted to leave. After all, I had healed the Nubrevnan. Now it was time to go.

I glared at the Rook—and at the man—but they were so wrapped up in crooning to each other, they didn't notice.

My glower deepened, and I slapped the leather kit onto the closest table. Yet before I could return the paper to its rightful place, I caught sight of a single word scrawled upon its edge.

MAP.

My mouth went dry. Could it be? Surely Sirmaya would not favor me so. In a crinkling flurry of speed, I unfolded the page.

And sure enough, my eyes landed upon a map of the mountain.

It was all there. This workshop, the ice pathway from before. Even the shadow wyrm nest was marked along with the all the tunnels and passageways I'd tried earlier.

None of that interested me, though. All I cared about was what waited ahead. The massive spiral on the bottom-most corner of the map that said *SUMMONING*.

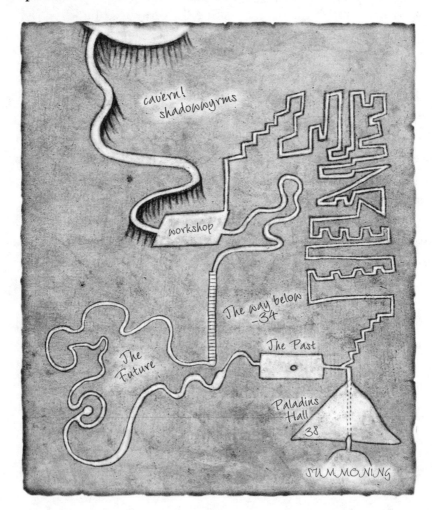

That was where the Sisters must go when Summoned, so *that* was where I needed to be.

My breaths turned shallow with excitement. There was a long route that would cut me all the way around, tunnel after tunnel, passage after passage, or there was a shortcut.

A blessed *shortcut* through a space labeled *Paladins' Hall*.

According to the map, crevices, cliffs, and dangerous drop-offs filled the triangular cavern, but I had an Airwitch at my side. And though he might not know how to use his magic now, I was certain we could figure it out by the time we reached this Paladins' Hall.

Grinning, I folded the map neatly back into shape and stowed it in a pocket right above my heart. Then I pinned my gaze on the Nubrevnan.

"I have to call you something," I declared, marching toward him. "So what will it be?"

His eyebrows ticked up a notch. He paused his scratching at the Rook's neck. "How about . . . your hero and savior? That has a nice tone to it—"

I smacked him on the head.

He laughed, which I had to admit was a nice sound. Though perhaps it was simply my own excitement brightening the moment.

"Are you always like this?" I asked as he stood, stiff yet surprisingly energetic. "Or is it the pain making you act this way? Or perhaps that tincture labeled Cure-All?"

"You mean, am I always this charming?"

"Ridiculous was more what I had in mind."

"You wound me, Ryber Fortiza." He reached a steadying hand to a table. "As for your question, I don't know if I'm always this way. I cannot remember a thing."

Again, the air turned frosty. My breath fogged.

"How about I call you Captain, then?" I pointed to his buttons. "That's what the silver means, isn't it?"

"Captain," he repeated, his gaze turning distant. "I suppose . . . hye, that will work." The faintest dusting of snow began to fall.

It landed on my face, a welcome cool against the scratches the Rook had left behind. And despite the sting on my cheeks, I grinned and grinned and grinned—for oh, yes, Sirmaya had blessed me indeed. A map and an Airwitch. I would reach my Sisters soon.

"Then let's go, Captain." I spread my arms wide. "Assuming you feel up to it, I've found a way out, and there's no time to waste."

"You mean you're bringing me with you?" The snow stopped in a heartbeat.

"Of course." I whirled around before I had to see his terrifying grin, and aiming for the stairs, I fastened the healer kit to my belt.

"I knew it!" Captain called after me.

I couldn't help it. I paused at the bottom step and glanced back. "What did you know?"

And there it was: his smile. Although . . . it didn't bother me as much this time.

"Admit it, Ryber Fortiza," he declared with a twirling hand. "You *do* think I'm charming."

※

Y2787 D106

MEMORIES

Lisbet returned from her Summoning today.

She appeared in the Grove as all Sisters do after meeting the Goddess, but there was something different about her. I sensed it the instant the rock slid back within the dolmen.

Power *coursed* off of her. It sent waves to dance upward through the dawn light. I do not think the other Sisters sensed it, for they do not work beside Sirmaya as I do. They are not accustomed to seeing Threads of power or sifting through them to grab hold.

Lisbet walked tranquilly toward me, her gait as smooth as that of the dancers whom the Exalted Ones so love to watch at midwinter.

Her eyes were more silver than I've ever seen. Almost transparent.

She strutted right past Sister Nadya, who always greets new Sightwitch Sisters, and came for me instead.

I must admit, I was frightened. I feared the power this little girl possessed, and I feared that somehow her time with Sirmaya had changed her.

But as soon as she reached me, she flung her arms around my waist and hugged, hugged, hugged. I melted to my knees and towed her in more tightly.

"We missed you," I whispered to her while the other Sisters watched. No one made a move to stop us, and Nadya looked more puzzled than upset.

"I know," Lisbet said simply. Then she drew back until our eyes met. Hers almost *hurt* to stare into.

So bright.

"I must gather things, Dysi, and I will need your help to do it. A map, your flint pouch, and healing supplies. We must place them in your workshop. Then you must build two new tools for me. A viewing glass that will allow us to see the past lives of the Paladins."

"And what else?" I pressed.

"A blade for killing them."

Gooseflesh prickled down my arms. I did not question for a moment that what she commanded did indeed need doing. Her words were not those of a child but of ancient, all-knowing truth.

However, I did ask, "Why, Lisbet? What have you seen?"

"I saw the last Sightwitch Sister go into the mountain. In a thousand years, she will pass through the halls with a Paladin at her side. We must prepare a path for her, Dysi, and we must get everything ready so she will not be lost."

"A thousand years." The words tasted like fire. They seemed to dry my throat just from the uttering.

Yes, Sightwitches lived in the future, but never—*never*—had I heard of a Sightwitch seeing so far ahead.

The chill bumps on my arms spread to my neck. "Why must we do it now, Lisbet? Why not ten years from now?"

"Because," she said, a sudden smile flashing over her face—so at odds with the words that came next—"none of us will be here in ten years, Dysi." She slid her hand into mine, and added, "Can we go see Cora now, please? Her throat should be all better, and she's been asking for us."

—— ✳ ——

3(?) hours left to find Tanzi—

Having company made the journey much better.

There.

I wrote it because it's true: having company made the journey better.

Yes, I was worried about Tanzi and the Sisters. Yes, I was trying to keep track of time's passage as best I could. And yes, I constantly had to hurry Captain along. But it was nice not to be alone.

Captain was fascinated by everything. He asked a thousand questions, like some newly arrived Serving Sister to the Convent.

In fact, just as I had with many a new Sister, I had to explain who the Sightwitches were, what our mission was, and why I was inside the mountain at all.

I told him everything. About our benevolent Goddess Sirmaya, about the Rules and the glamour, about how I had been the only Sister left. I told him that, despite thirteen years here, I'd never been Summoned inside the mountain.

He was so easy to talk to, and for a man with an injured chest and no memories, he was a surprisingly good listener. His sympathetic grunts and occasional oaths sounded genuine, and the sudden snow that fluttered around us made me think he truly felt my plight.

"How do you speak Nubrevnan so well?" he asked at one point as we tromped down a square stairwell marked on the map as simply *The Way Below* and with a little *34* scribbled next to it.

Thank the Sleeper there were Firewitched lanterns to light our way since I'd lost my own when I'd lost the pack. They winked into power without any command. We would reach ten paces away and *whoof!* the next lantern would flash to life.

"We learn all the languages of the Witchlands," I explained. Step, step, step. "We begin by learning songs, so that the melodies help stick new syllables and sounds into our minds."

"Let me guess. You started with 'The Maidens North of Lovats.'"

"It was the third song, actually." I glanced back, impressed. "How did you guess?"

"Because 'blighter' isn't a real word—and you've used it twice now."

"Not a real word? Then why is it in the song?"

"I don't know. For rhythm's sake, perhaps?" And then, absolutely unbidden, he splayed a graceful hand to his chest—the unharmed part—and began to sing. "The Maidens north of Lovats, none ever looked so fair—"

"No!" I swung around, palms rising. "No singing! Who knows what creatures are in here that you might wake up?"

Captain's face sank. Then he turned to the Rook, who'd been riding on his massive shoulder this whole time. "I wasn't that loud, was I, Rook? *Ow.*" He swatted the bird off his shoulder. "He bit me!"

"Of course he did." I fought to keep my face set firmly in a frown. "His name is *the* Rook, not just Rook."

"The 'the' is that important, is it?" He rubbed at his ear and pouted like a sullen child the size of a tree trunk. Even his wrists and ears were enormous.

When the air around us warmed with a charged heat, a delight sifted through me. Captain was finding his magic again. It was only a matter of time before he remembered how to use it.

"The 'the,'" I said, resuming the hike, "is as important as the lack of a 'ta' in my name. Ryber, not Ryber*ta*. *The* Rook, not Rook."

"But you're a person," Captain argued, his footsteps resuming behind me. "It's a bird."

"*He's* a bird," I corrected.

"Noden save me—you really don't ever break the rules, do you?"

"What does that mean?" Heat fanned up my cheeks. How did he know I liked rules so much? He'd only known me a few hours.

I almost wish I hadn't asked the question, for he proceeded to describe in explicit detail (what an ability for recall considering he had no memory!) every single rule I'd told him to follow since leaving the workshop—as well as every single time I'd scolded him for not following said rules.

"Forty-three times," he told me. "Hye, I counted, and I'd say there's no denying that you really love your rules."

"I don't *love* them," I muttered. "But why have them if you aren't going to follow them?"

"Or," he countered, picking up his pace and falling into step beside me, "maybe rules exist simply for the breaking."

My chest tightened at those words. He sounded exactly like Tanzi, and the only way I could hide the sudden tears burning behind my eyes was to offer him the same answer I'd always given her.

Though first, I offered a hard scoff. "I like rules." I stomped a bit faster. "They give me structure. They give me a clear path to follow—which is Rule 15, by the way: Always follow the marked path."

"But maybe the marked path isn't the right one. Maybe," he dragged out that word as if still thinking, "there isn't one set path at all."

"Of course there is. There are no coincidences, and there is no changing what is meant to be."

"But how do you *know* that? How do you know all of this"—he twirled his hand—"is what you're meant to be and not something else?"

I skidded to a halt so fast I almost tripped—and for some reason I really can't explain, a fury rose inside me. A boiling, vicious heat that I could convey only in a single word, "*What?*"

Captain took the question exactly as spoken. "I asked how you knew that—"

"I heard you, but why would you say that?"

"Well, you said you are the only Sister without the Sight, which has me thinking: maybe that's simply not what you're meant to be."

"Of *course* it's what I'm meant to be," I gnashed out. "There are no coincidences! I found the Convent on my own when I was only four years old. I'm the only Sister ever to do that! Which means Sirmaya brought me here because this what I'm meant to be. A Sightwitch Sister. A *powerful* Sightwitch Sister. End of story."

As I kicked into a raging stomp, hands shaking at my sides, a tremor struck. Stronger than before, it stole my feet from under me.

I crumpled to the steps, curled in a ball with my hands over my head, and waited for the quake to pass.

It lasted for at least a minute, the mountain grinding and furious. Dust puffed and plumed. Stones roared against stones.

Sirmaya is angry. It was the only thought I could produce. *Sirmaya is angry. Sirmaya is angry.*

I just prayed she wasn't angry with me. I had forced my way into the mountain, and I had broken more rules than I could count.

When at last the shaking subsided, I didn't move right away. I simply lay there, wound up and with my pulse thumping in my ears.

Had I made a mistake? Was the Goddess angry because I had chosen the wrong path?

No, I decided at last. Captain was wrong. There were no coincidences, and this was my path.

I would finish what I had come to do. I would find Tanzi and the other Sisters, and no matter what might happen, I had to stay firmly gripped upon that.

Y2787 D176

MEMORIES

Something Lisbet said this morning has altered everything. One comment, and my entire perspective has changed.

I was showing her my latest design for the viewing glass and blade.

"The glass must be bigger." She pointed at the frame.

"Glass is expensive," I said, more than a little annoyed. This was, after all, my fourth design that an *eight-year-old* had turned down. "Not to mention, it's very hard to buy in the middle of a mountain range, Lisbet."

"Bigger," she insisted.

"The power from Sirmaya is strong," I insisted back. "I do not see why we must lose more time and money on a larger piece of glass."

Her little jaw jutted sideways, and I swear her eyes flashed with silver light. "It does not matter if Sirmaya is strong," she said with all the authority of the Goddess. "If Her Threads do not have enough surface to bind to, then the spell will never be powerful enough."

My mouth fell open. I gawked like a fool for at least an entire minute while the implications of her words unraveled in my mind.

Of course. Of *course* a spell to reveal a Paladin's past lives would need heaps of power, and of course the Threads of that power would need space to adhere to.

All this time, it was not that the Vergedi Knot hadn't been strong enough to create a passageway; I had been using materials *too small*.

Blessed Sirmaya, why had I not seen? It was so obvious! The answer had been lurking beneath my toe all along, but I had never once thought to lift my foot.

"Right," I mumbled at her, already turning away. Already shooting for the stairs. "I'll have Nadya send for more glass." My feet hit the steps, and I barreled downstairs to my piles of rock. Limestone from the coast, granite from these mountains, clay from the plains in the North . . .

Six types of stone for the six doorways I needed to build. But small rocks would not do. I needed boulders. I needed monoliths.

Saria, I decided before I even reached the closest pile. Lady Saria would be able to help, and I had a meeting in a week with the Six.

It was all going to *work*.

And Sister Nadya had been right this whole time: all I had needed to find my answer was a change to shake things loose.

———— ✳ ————

2(?) hours left to find Tanzi

Captain tried to apologize. It was the only time we spoke for the rest of our trek on the Way Below—and also the only words we shared in a tunnel carved entirely through ice labeled *The Future*.

Seventeen times Captain declared he was sorry, and seventeen times I ignored him.

It was childish of me. I see that now, but responding meant I would have to consider why his words upset me.

And that was something I was not ready to do.

The Rook nestled on my shoulder the whole journey, and each time my teeth started chattering, he cuddled against my neck.

Like before, in the cavern with the shadow wyrms, the ice seemed lit from within. It glowed so bright I had to squint to see.

And also like before, black filaments and patches hovered deep within the frozen blue. Too far away to distinguish real shapes, but they were there all the same and impossible to ignore.

"What do you think they are?" Captain asked as we hurried past one dark expanse that was faintly human in shape. Lines radiated out from it in all directions. "It almost looks like the ice is . . . is *cleaving*."

"You remember what cleaving is," I said flatly, speaking to him for the first time in at least half an hour, "but not your own name?"

He shrugged one shoulder. "I don't understand it either. I know how to hold a knife properly and I can sing all the words to 'The Maidens North of Lovats.' But what my name is or how I got here or why I'm covered in this foul gunk"—he swatted at his sleeves—"I cannot recall at all."

A beat passed. Two. Then he added hastily, "I'm sorry. I didn't mean to upset you before."

Apology number eighteen, and this time I offered a grunt in return.

Ninety-three steps later, we left the Future and reached a new spot on the map: a long, dark room labeled *The Past*.

"Strange names," Captain whispered as he read the map over my shoulder. "Sort of morbid, don't you think?"

"The Sightwitches love their symbolism," I replied—also a whisper, for this space demanded quiet. Then, because I didn't know what else to do, I murmured, "Ignite."

A small puff sounded, and a lone torch burst into life on the wall beside us. It was the only one like it. So I crept over, Captain just behind, and hauled it out.

The Rook didn't appreciate the bouncing of my shoulder, so after an ornery hiss in my ear—even *he* stayed quiet in this room—he hopped back to Captain's broader roosting spot.

The torch fit perfectly in my hand. Exactly the right size for my fingers to grip comfortably, exactly the right weight for me to hold without my arm tiring.

"What do these marks mean?" Captain asked, and when I swung the light where he pointed, a stark relief came into view.

It was the same motif from the tunnels, but carved above every tenth stone was a new design.

"They're . . . mason marks," I said slowly, the memory of a lesson with Hilga unfurling. "Which means this room was built before the time of Earthwitches."

"I didn't know there was a time before Earthwitches."

"Because people have forgotten. It was a time before magic existed everywhere in the Witchlands." Keeping the wall at my side, I resumed our walk onward. This time, Captain stayed next to me and I didn't stop him. The darkness in this room felt alive. It breathed and prowled, and the only weapon we had was the torch's weak flicker.

If not for the map, I would have had no way to know the room's shape was rectangular or that an exit waited at the room's opposite end.

"When the Sightwitches hid behind the glamour," I explained in soft tones, "all the records and memories we'd kept were soon forgotten, for history is all too easily rewritten and the past is all too easily erased."

Just as I had done in the Way Below, I slipped into my role of teacher. Reciting lessons and sharing what I knew—something about that simple task made the endless black around us seem less threatening.

And just as I had memorized every rule word for word, I had memorized this lesson *exactly* as Sister Hilga had taught it to me.

"Once, there were only twelve people in all the Witchlands with magic. Known as the Paladins, they were gifted their powers by the sleeping Goddess Herself and tasked with protecting the land. When a Paladin died, his or her memories and magic were reborn in another. Over and over again, this cycle continued for as long as the Witchlands existed. Until one day, the Twelve disappeared."

Cold whispered over me—a gust from Captain's magic. "Where did the Paladins go?" he asked.

"They died forever. No more reincarnation." I ran my hand over the motif as I walked, its grooves surprisingly warm to the touch. Then I recited:

"Six turned on six and made themselves kings.
One turned on five, and stole everything."

"I've heard that before," Captain murmured. He rubbed at his brow. "It's from . . . something."

I nodded. "'Eridysi's Lament.' Though I'm surprised you've heard that part. Most people only know one tiny verse."

"About a broken heart, isn't it? For some reason, I remember that song too. But don't worry. I won't sing it." Captain scratched at the Rook, who didn't offer his usual croon at the attention. "But the lines that you quoted—what do they mean?"

"They mean that the Paladins turned on each other. After millennia of watching leaders rise and fall, of maintaining peace and living on the fringes of society, half of the Paladins decided they wanted power. They wanted to lead. So six killed six, and then one final Paladin betrayed them all . . ." I trailed off as Captain vanished from the torch's light.

He had stopped walking.

"What is it?" I angled back. Light washed over him. "What's wrong?"

His head was cocked to one side, his eyes thinned. A breath passed before he whispered, "Do you hear that?"

My fingers moved for my knife. "Hear what?"

He surveyed the center of the room, but there was nothing to see beyond shadows.

"Voices," Captain said at last. "Do you hear them speaking to us?"

"No," I said, "and you probably shouldn't listen." Already he'd set off, though. With no worry at all, his long legs carried him away and the darkness pulled him in.

My stomach hollowed out. My mouth went dry, but against all reason or logic, I pushed into a scamper after him.

He took one loping step for each of my three. Soon enough, though, I and my torchlight caught up. He was planted before a marble pedestal, on which a hilt rested, almost as long as my forearm but with only a jagged fragment of steel to jut above the cross-guard.

And beside the broken blade was a square frame with a long handle. It reminded me of a reading glass used to magnify small text, except that this frame was larger and most of its glass had been shattered and lost.

Before I could stop Captain, his fingers had curled around the glass's handle. He was lifting it high. I grabbed for his arm, but I was too late. Too slow.

Then I saw him. Through the shards still clinging to the frame's edge, I saw him. I ripped my hand back and clutched my throat.

For it was not Captain's face that appeared through the glass. It was a scarred face, a furious face. A man with his lips curled back and teeth bared in violence.

I reeled back two steps, and the face changed to a woman's. Then another man's. Then too fast to tell, I saw one person blur into the next—each as vicious and wrathful as the last.

Then Captain dropped the glass, and his hands clutched at his face. "Stop," he snarled. "I can't understand you—"

He broke off, whipping around. Then he shouted into the darkness, "Who are you? Show yourselves!" He spun again, louder and louder with each cry. "Stop shouting at me—who are you? Stop, stop, *stop*."

He fell to his knees in a great crunch of bone that rattled through the tiles. His movement turned jerky and frantic.

I did not know what to do. My feet were stuck to the floor, and my mind had shrunk down to a useless pinprick of thought: *What is happening to him?*

I got my answer mere moments later when he lurched right for me.

"Kill me." The words razored from his throat. His eyes bulged, glittering orbs in the dim circle of light. "KILL ME."

Black lines radiated across his face and into his eyes. One black bubble built at the edge of his jaw.

I didn't think—there was no time for it. All I could do was react. He was cleaving, his magic was burning through him, and if I didn't do *something* right now, he would kill me.

I had not seen cleaving before, but I had read about it often enough to know death was the only outcome.

I flung the torch at him. It shuddered through the air, and before I saw it land, I was at the pedestal and hauling up the massive hilt. It took both my hands to grip it, but that shorn steel jutting up was still long enough to slice.

And long enough, I hoped, to kill.

I rounded back toward him. On his hands and knees, he had already crawled past the torch. It burned behind him, silhouetting him in flame.

He looked like Skull-Face from the Crypts.

I attacked. I *had* to—he was too large for me to fight if I didn't get him while he was low. So I aimed for his face, and I charged.

In two leaping steps, I was to him. He tipped back his head, as if offering me his throat.

"Kill me," he repeated. No longer a rasp, but a clear, insistent command that coursed straight to the center of my mind.

I stumbled. I slowed. I hesitated.

And in that moment, the Rook dove between us. Feathers and howling and talons to slice. The attack he had threatened in the workshop he now gave in full force.

His claws slashed my face, his power drove me back. The blade fell from my hands in a clatter of metal. I rocked back, arms flailing—but not enough to keep me from crashing to the floor.

Then everything stopped. The Rook flapped to Captain, who now lay sprawled across the tiles, and for several booming heartbeats, I sat there and did not move.

My wrists ached from breaking my fall. My face burned with lines of throbbing heat, where each of the Rook's talons had torn skin.

Meanwhile, the torch flickered on and on, shadows to undulate over Captain. Darkness thrummed around me. I was outside the light's reach; I could hear nothing but my own shallow breaths and slamming pulse.

"I'm sorry." The words slid over the tiles to me. Captain rolled to his side, the movement stiff. Pained. With the torch behind him, I couldn't see his face. "I . . . am so sorry, Ryber."

The Rook nudged Captain's leg, purring with concern.

"What are you?" I breathed, my body still as stone.

"I don't know." With a harsh exhale, he pushed into a sitting position.

The light behind him shrank even more, and the Rook hopped around to Captain's leg.

Twice now, the bird had chosen this Nubrevnan man over me. Yet I was neither upset nor angry.

The Rook did nothing without reason, so the question was: What was his reason?

"You cleaved," I said, finally drawing in my legs as if to rise.

Captain nodded slowly. It sent the light bouncing. "But then the cleaving stopped."

"That's not possible." I knew it wasn't possible. Sister Hilga and Sister Rose both had taught me that, and I'd read it in Memory Records too.

"But it did." He mimicked me, pulling in his own legs. "A voice told me, 'Not yet,' and then the . . . the *fire* in my veins went away."

Though my wrists groaned in protest, I pushed myself to my feet. "The voices you heard before the cleaving—who were they? *What* were they?"

"I don't know." He wagged his head, and as he continued to speak, I approached him, one measured step at a time.

I kept my hand on my knife the whole way.

"They used words I didn't understand, Ryber, and they screamed and screamed and screamed. They were hurting. Someone had . . . had betrayed them. That much I knew—that much I could feel. Except that it also felt like *me*. Like the voices were *my* memories and I had been betrayed."

I reached Captain's side, and as one, he and the Rook lifted their gazes to me.

The Rook bristled, a challenge glittering in his eyes.

Captain, however, looked so deeply ashamed, so deeply sorry, I thought he might ask me again to kill him.

We held each other's gaze, his chest unmoving. Mine bowing in and out. Three breaths I took. Then he said, "I don't like this place, Ryber. I want to leave. After we find your Sisters, please: I want to leave."

It took me a moment to gather my words. The truth was that I didn't know how to leave. I didn't know what would happen once I found Tanzi and the others. For all I knew, I would join them.

And at my core, that was certainly what I hoped for.

So I answered simply, "We're almost there, Captain." Then I extended my hand to him.

He tensed at the movement. Then he seemed to realize what it meant—that I was not only allowing him physical contact, but I was offering it.

The edge of his lip twitched upward, but he didn't take my hand in his. Instead he lumbered to a stand on his own—which I appreciated. After retrieving the torch, I found him hunched, a pillar of shame with the Rook resting on his shoulder.

"If it happens again," he said. "If I cleave again, please stab me with your knife, Ryber. I don't ever want to frighten you, and I don't ever want to hurt you."

"Hye," I said, though I stared at the Rook as I said it.

For we both knew he would never let me kill Captain. There was something special about this Nubrevnan man, and I had my suspicions of what that might be.

—— ✳ ——

Y2787 D271

MEMORIES

For once, all of the Six were present at today's meeting in my work-shop. Not that the Rook King contributed much. 'Tis strange how he sits at our table and speaks when spoken to, yet he never feels as if he is *part* of the group.

This whole enterprise was his idea, so of course he is part of it. Of course, he is one of us.

Yet this feeling nags. Plus, I'm often left wondering when I will meet his general. If this man is so important to our plans, then why does he never come?

Like before, Lady Baile tarried after the meeting, waiting until all the others had left. I knew what she would ask before her lips could even part, and I flushed to my toes at the prospect of it.

So before she could utter a word, I blurted, "How did you know Bastien was your Heart-Thread?"

Her pale eyebrows sprang high. "The wise Sightwitch asking me for advice? What a strange twist."

Heat burned hotter on my cheeks, and she laughed. "I should not tease, Dysi. My apologies. And to answer your question"—she leaned onto the edge of the table and patted at her heart—"I knew Bastien was the one for me because I felt it here."

"Was he your Heart-Thread in . . . past lives?" I hesitated with that question. The Paladins spoke rarely of their reincarnations, and

I've never known if it was because the subject was uncomfortable or if they'd simply forgotten that this body was not the one they'd always had.

Judging by Baile's easy response, I decided it was the latter.

"No, he was not my Heart-Thread in past lives. And perhaps he never will be again. Heart-Threads are not fated, nor are they necessarily singular. Like any relationship, a Heart-Thread is a choice you make.

"The bond forms from respect and shared experience, and though attraction can sometimes play its part, it is not necessary. Love is love, and is the most powerful connection we humans have."

She paused, her lips pursing to one side. Yet again, my blush would not abate, and I found myself glancing down at my hands like some child trying to impress her mother.

"Dysi," she murmured at last, and with a gentle flick of her finger, she tipped up my chin. Then she offered me the smile of one who has lived a thousand lives and loved a thousand loves. "If you have found someone you care about," she said, "and if that person cares for you in return, do not let it slip past. It will be your greatest regret if you do."

She withdrew her hand, and before I could summon a worthy response, she rose from the table and our meeting was officially over.

1(?) hour left to find Tanzi—

Paladins' Hall.

If I had thought the lair of the shadow wyrms massive, it was nothing compared to this cavern. For as far as I could see, the ceiling crooked up and up and up.

And for as far as I could see, it plummeted down.

Captain and I stood on a crooked outcropping, the tunnel we'd just abandoned at our backs.

There was nowhere to go save for a stairwell charging up to our left. Yet the map clearly showed seven doorways at different levels and depths, as well as a path straight through the hall's center.

"I expected a bridge," I said, stretching the map wide and holding it before me. "See? Right here, it says a bridge will take us up to the door I need."

As I spoke, the Rook rubbed his beak against my ear. I absently scratched at his neck. "See anything useful?" I asked him, but all he did was coo.

"Maybe the bridge fell?" Captain suggested. He strutted to the rocky edge. A tilt of his long body, a stretch of his neck, and he peered straight down.

I shuddered. "You're making me nervous bending over the edge like that."

"I am rather close, aren't I?" He flipped his smudged hand in my direction, flashing his Witchmark. "I think my body knows it can fly, even if my mind says, 'Absolutely not.'" With that, he straightened and declared, "There's nothing to see anyway. Whatever bridge there was, it isn't here now."

I sent a frown up the stairs. The map showed a doorway up there, but it was not the one I needed. In fact, it distinctly said *No* beside it.

But there was no alternative, and every moment Captain and I stood here was one less moment I had to reach Tanzi.

Time was running out. I didn't know precisely how long I had left, but I knew it couldn't be much.

So up the steps we went, the Rook by wing and Captain and I by foot. Fifty-four steps in total, each one uneven and awkwardly steep.

Captain found the steps an easy height, yet even he was panting by the time we reached the top—where we faced a second uneven outcropping as well as the door marked on the map.

It was not a true door but rather an archway twice my height and four times my width. Gray rubble blocked half of it, as if a brick wall had been destroyed on the other side.

Everything within the archway glowed with the faintest blue light, and I'd have thought it from the ice or the foxfire had there actually been any nearby. But there wasn't. Instead, the cavern wall was empty save for six fat sconces stacked on either side of the ledge. They all burst into fiery life as soon as my feet left the final stair.

I froze midstep, as did Captain. We stood there, braced for shadow wyrms or voices or Death Maidens to sing.

The Rook, however, seemed as bored as bored could be. He hopped and pecked around the fallen bricks as if hunting spiders—except I knew he would never deign to eat a spider.

I didn't trust his complacency, though, so with measured steps, I crept toward the doorway. With each inch, sounds trickled in. Frogs, crickets, a breeze . . . and something else. Something that buzzed atop it all and shivered in my teeth.

"Cicadas." The word popped from Captain's mouth, seeming to surprise him almost as much as it surprised me.

"But we don't have cicadas here," I said. "And . . . are these tree roots?" Curiosity dashed away my caution. I strode over and touched the gnarled plant that twined around the rubble. It was tough, but more bark-like than root-like.

"It's a grapevine," Captain said, a puzzled lilt to his voice. "And *that* is my button."

I swung around to face him, and sure enough, the Rook had a silver button clenched in his beak.

My forehead scrunched up. "You must have come this way. But how? And where does this door even go?"

Captain shrugged, but it was a distracted movement. Already, he was darting past me, aiming for the rubble and the vines.

"I don't remember being here," he said, "but these sounds, this breeze. I do know them. Which means . . ." He bent forward, hands splaying on the stones. "It means I ought to go through, don't you think?"

He lifted one leg as if to climb—

"No." The word slashed out, and I lurched at him. With the movement came Tanzi's face and Hilga's frown and the shattered hourglass. All of it roared through me in a punch of stomach-stealing fear.

I was out of time.

"You can't go that way." I thrust the map at him. "It very clearly says 'No,' and besides . . . I . . ."

"You what?" He scrutinized me, and for half a moment, as the blue off the archway pulsed over us both, I was hit with the sense of falling.

Just a whoosh of air and a sharp pop in my ears.

Then it passed, and I was left blinking as the words, "There is no bridge," fell from my tongue.

"No bridge," Captain repeated slowly. He too, I thought, had felt that strange punch of vertigo.

But then my words seemed to settle in his brain, and he straightened up off the stones, breaking free from my grasp.

"I see," he murmured. A halo of snow fluttered to life around his head. "You want me to fly you somewhere, even though I don't know how."

"You *do*," I countered. "The magic is still in you."

"If that were true, then don't you think I would have summoned it against the shadow wryms?"

"You're using it right now!" I pointed, and the map—still clutched tight—crinkled in my hand. "That snow is from you!"

He glanced left, right, and his widening eyes told me that until that moment, he hadn't even noticed the snow. All this time, he'd been changing the temperature, and he hadn't even realized.

"I . . . don't think . . ." He shook his head. "I don't think I'm doing this."

"You *are*."

"Then I don't know how!" Captain backed away, almost tripping over the Rook who hopped and squawked.

The snow chased after, and this time, the faintest wind gusted up from Captain's toes.

What little color he possessed leached entirely from his face.

"Magic is what makes a person cleave." He clasped his arms to his chest, as if he could keep the wind and the snow at bay. "If I try to use this power, I might cleave again. Then what?"

My lips parted. I sucked in air, ready to answer . . .

But then my mouth clamped shut. For there was nothing I could say. If he cleaved, then one of us would die. That was that.

"I thought so." His arms relaxed, and the snow broke off. Not the wind, though. It funneled around him and whipped against me.

Hot, dry, *powerful* wind.

"I won't let you risk it, Ryber. I won't let you endanger your life just so you can go deeper into this nightmare place." He drew himself up to his fullest height, a towering beast of a man, and there was a clear challenge in his jaw.

I was having none of it.

I matched his posture. I matched his expression. Then I marched right up to him and poked him in the shoulder. "Don't," I hissed, "say 'just.' I do not want your magic *just* so I can go deeper into the mountain. I go after my family, Captain. After my Threadsister.

"You may not remember anything, but surely you know what love and loyalty feel like. So do not tell me that if your family, that if your best friend in the *entire universe* needed you, you would give up on them.

"All I'm asking is that you fly me to this ledge." I shook the map in his face. "Then you can leave. You can go right through this door and figure out who you are."

So certain was I that he would argue more—so *sure* was I that he would shout or make a run for the archway—that I planted my feet and braced for impact.

Instead, his chin dropped, and he said, "Fine." Then he spun away and marched to the outcropping's edge.

My jaw sank low, and when I glanced at the Rook, he looked as shocked as I, his beak half open and head dipped to one side.

"Well?" Captain called. "Are you coming or not?"

"Right." I scurried over, and before he could change his mind, I flung my arms around him.

"Uh." He cleared his throat, and the air around us ratcheted up to boiling. "Why are you holding me?"

"For flying."

"The thing is, you, uh . . . You don't need to."

I flung off my arms and tumbled back. Heat that was not from his magic flagged through me.

"Not that I mind, of course," he added hastily, amusement crinkling his eyes, "but surely I can create multiple air currents. Seems logical, right? And the two separate currents will get us where we're going—and where is that, by the way?"

Embarrassment blazed onto my neck and cheeks as I pointed vaguely up. "Somewhere that way. And stop smiling."

His grin stretched wider. "I'm not smiling. This is simply my summoning-magic face."

"Liar," I muttered. Then, for good measure, I added, "Blighter." But the word was lost in a roar of wind that tore around me. It curled beneath my feet, a physical thing that grabbed my arms, my legs, my waist.

I rocketed up, the stone fell away, and the next thing I knew, I was flying.

I might have been screaming too, but my voice was lost in the charged, spinning air that grasped me. My stomach was lost as well, left on the stone below where it could vomit up bile without me.

And my heart—blessed Sirmaya, it was going to explode in my eardrums if we didn't slow or return to the ground or . . . *something*.

At least the wind was too strong for me to look down, though, and see how far we had to fall.

As I tried to swivel my head to see Captain, something fizzy surged up from my belly and curled into my skull. It sang along the back of my neck and behind my ribs.

I was flying. *I was flying.*

Captain had done it, and any moment now, we would land and I could finally, finally reach my Sisters.

—— ✳ ——

Y2787 D336

MEMORIES

The first doorway is complete.

I did it.

I cannot believe it, but the magic path stands directly before me as I write this, sitting on the cold floor in Saria's carved hall.

The Rook King was the first of the Six to get me a boulder. Less than a day since our meeting, and the monolith arrived on a wagon hauled by twelve horses. We set it up in the meadow west of the river, where the earth dips low and Sirmaya's power rises up from the soil.

It was simply too awkward to get the stone into the mountain itself, and just as I had speculated, I didn't need to. The spell worked fine aboveground, and all the Threads bound exactly as they should.

From Goddess to boulder to doorway.

Now the question is: Do I dare walk through?

—— ✳ ——

1/2 hour(?) left to find Tanzi

Our landing was not as graceful as our takeoff.

The ledge and door that the map led us to were easy to find—exactly where I'd pointed, and, like before, sconces whuffed to life at our approach.

An approach that was not slowing down. The light from the lanterns flared into six orange lines.

"Too fast!" I bellowed over the winds, but either Captain didn't hear or didn't care. "Too fast!" I tried again, shrieking now. We were going to hit that rock at full speed. "Too fast, too fast, TOO FAST—"

We slammed to the ground. My ankles crunched, my knees buckled. I crashed forward, hands catching me for the second time that day in a wrist-popping finish.

But there was no time to notice the pain. No spare thought to waste on it. I staggered to my feet and aimed for the door that had been marked on the map.

Identical to the entry into the Crypts and the workshop, a knife-sized slot waited just ahead. Vaguely, I was aware of the Rook joining us—with a far more graceful landing—and of Captain behind me, laughing, clapping, and declaring, "I did it! Did you see, Ryber? I just flew us over that chasm!"

Captain and the Rook were unimportant, though. Dim and distant. Nothing mattered but opening this door.

And praying that time had not yet run out.

Breath held and hand shaking, I slid the knife in. A rasp of metal on granite. Then a click, a shudder to ripple outward, as the doorway split. A pale glow sliced down the center and two panels swung back.

Ice met my eyes.

More cursed ice.

I don't know precisely what I'd expected. The map had said *SUM-MONING*, so I'd envisioned something vaguely glorious. Something to make all this horror and heartache worth it.

Instead, there was simply more ice like we'd seen throughout, with shadows and black webs hovering inside. Fog skated across my boots.

Unlike before, however, the passage that cut forward was a mere crack in the cold. So narrow and low, I would have to walk with head bowed and shoulders angled sideways.

"That's a tight fit," Captain said, and I flinched.

I'd forgotten he was here.

Frowning, I sheathed my knife. "You don't have to fit," I told him. "You can leave now, Captain. You flew me here, and now . . . You can leave this 'nightmare place' and find out where you came from."

Eyes thinned, he glanced from me to the door. Then back to me again. "It doesn't look very safe in there. What if you get hurt?"

"My Sisters will help," I said, though I had no idea if it was true. Nor did I care. Time was moving forward while I stayed still.

"I can take care of myself," I added, lifting my arm. "Come on, the Rook."

After a sympathetic cluck in Captain's direction, the Rook obeyed. A flap, a swoop, and his weight bore down on my forearm. Then hop, hop, hop he reached my shoulder.

"Will I see you again?" Captain asked, and I made the mistake of meeting his gaze. Of taking in his face.

"Wounded" is the only word I can think of to describe it. His ribs bowed in, out, each breath short and rasping.

All while snowflakes danced around his head.

"I don't know," I answered honestly.

"I could wait for you." His eyebrows crooked up in earnest. "Then we could leave this place together."

I shook my head, a single curt movement. "I'm not sure I'll be coming back, Captain. I . . ." I glanced at the Rook. Then at my toes. Anywhere to avoid meeting his sad, sad eyes. "I'm not sure what I'll find inside here or how long it will take me. You should leave, while you have the chance."

Then, because I had no choice, I turned away from him. "I'm sorry, Captain. I have to go now."

"Oh." The word was more sigh than tangible sound, and a whip of cold air kissed my shoulders as I strode away.

"Good-bye," I said, and I did not look back.

When I reached the ice, I bent low. A dip of my torso, a slouch of my spine, and I ducked into the ice.

The last thing I heard before the passage swerved left and the ice swallowed me entirely was a gentle, "Thank you for saving me, Ryber Fortiza, and I hope you find what you're looking for."

Navigating the ice took all my concentration and all my flexibility. The path leaned and dipped, warped and contorted.

Within ten paces, the Rook had to abandon his spot on my shoulder and hop his way through. Another twenty paces, and the ice narrowed so tightly I had to squirm sideways, suck in my stomach, and shimmy onward.

The black shapes hovered, unmissable with my gaze aimed straight into the ice, and I had the strangest sense that the black lines tendriling outward were reaching for me.

Fortunately, the squeeze lasted only fifteen sideways steps. Then I popped into a room of such crystal perfection I could do nothing but stare for several long, shivering heartbeats.

The ice spun upward like a snail's spiral, and a pathway, smooth as glass, arched around the edge. Every few paces, an ice-clogged door honeycombed into the ice.

A crack erupted behind me. I jolted around, certain the ice had somehow moved. Certain the passage had collapsed behind me.

But it was just the Rook, shaking loose from the ice and clacking his displeasure. A frosty moment later, he resumed his perch atop my shoulder—and I resumed my journey forward.

Though I *did* wonder how the Rook had managed to make so much noise.

I quickly forgot my confusion. Up my feet carried me, careful at first in case the ice was slick. All was fine, though, and within one loop, I was running.

Then sprinting flat out. My arms swung, and I pumped my knees higher, faster. Around, around. Up, up.

My exhales came in sharp, cloudy gasps, and the Rook's talons dug deep to hold on. It hurt. I didn't care. I was too close to care about anything except slamming my feet, one foot after the next.

Had the Rook not stabbed his beak into my ear and screeched, I would never have noticed the gap in the ice. It was an open door.

I skidded to a stop, hand slinging out to wrench me back the other way.

My shredded palm tore anew.

"This . . . way?" I panted, and at the Rook's acknowledging purr, I shoved inside.

Except it wasn't the right way at all. I had entered a tiny cube room, where two shadows floated in the ice directly before me. Small shadows. Child-size.

Then, gouged out of the walls on either side of me were two holes, each my height and deep enough to hold me.

Before I could ask the Rook why we were here, he bounded off my shoulder with a squawk and landed beside a tattered book and a hand-size gold leather pouch.

Clearly, whatever these items were, he thought I needed them. "Fine," I huffed, trying to catch my breath.

I yanked up the pouch, but before I could snag the book, my eyes landed on its cover.

Diary of Eridysi Gochienka

My fogging breaths broke off. All I could do was stare, hand out-stretched. Body half crouched.

Eridysi Gochienka.

That was *the* Eridysi of legend, and this was her diary. Yet I felt no interest or elation at the sight of it. All that came was a vast shoveling horror.

For if this was her diary, then this place must be her tomb.

And if this was her tomb, then I knew what the shapes in the ice were—and I knew exactly why time was running out. The Sisters *had* been called for sleeping, and I had to reach their tombs before it was too late.

My muscles erupted with power. I snatched up the diary and pouch, and, abandoning the Rook, I charged out of the room and onto the spiral once more. Somehow my feet knew where to take me. Or perhaps it was Sirmaya, leading me the rest of the way.

The spiral blurred around me. I lost track of the cold, of the diary and pouch still clasped in my hands—of who I was at all. Everything shrank down to what I knew waited ahead.

After an eternity of running, I reached a gap in the ice large enough to barrel through. The spiral kept rising, but I *knew* this was the branch I needed.

I veered through it, and moments later, another cube faced me. This one, though, was large enough to hold a hundred Sisters.

Large enough to hold all the people I'd ever loved.

Then there they were. Each and every face of each and every Sightwitch who had filled my days. The ice hadn't covered them entirely yet—not all of them, at least. Some still had enough of their faces exposed for me to recognize them.

Over there was Ute, and beside her was Birgit. There were Rose and Trina and Margrette. Oriya and Fazimeh.

And there, in the farthest corner, was Hilga . . . with Tanzi right beside her.

I hurried to my Threadsister, a numbness rushing over me as I scanned the ice. There had to be a way to clear it. A way to dig her out—to dig them all out.

I rushed past Ute, then Birgit. They looked so peaceful with their eyes closed. Nothing like the images in the scrying pool.

Still, I had to *try* to break them free.

I reached Tanzi and dropped the diary and the pouch at my feet. "Wake up," I whispered. "Wake up, Tanz. I'm here—just like you asked. Please, wake up."

Nothing happened.

So with hands that trembled out of control, I unfastened my knife. It was the only tool I had for breaking the ice; it would have to be enough.

"Wake up," I said, louder now and, with my arm rearing back.

I stabbed the ice.

A shockwave tore out. It threw me backward, yanking me to the ground with mind-crunching power.

My head banged the ice. The world went black, and for a moment, I simply lay there.

Lost. No sound, no sight. I was stripped down to my barest nothing, and it took all I had to simply cling to consciousness.

I thought perhaps I had died.

But then my breath returned, aching and weak, followed by a flickering haze of glowing blue.

Last came sound. Words from throats I knew.

"She is dying," croaked Sister Rose.

"The Goddess is dying," said Ute. And Trina and Margrette and all the rest. "The Goddess is dying, the Goddess is dying."

Then loudest came Hilga's stern tone. It cut straight to my heart, and tears scorched in my eyes.

"Join us," Hilga said. "Join us in sleep, Ryber. Sirmaya needs us. We must give her our power so she can heal."

"But I have no power." The words cracked over my lips, and with a grunt to rattle even the Sleeper herself, I thrust myself up.

The Sisters' eyes were open now, mouths moving. "She is dying, Ryber. The Goddess is dying."

Only one Sister did not speak. The one I wanted most to hear from.

"Come," Hilga declared, her silver eyes locked on me. "You do not need the gift of Sight to help our Goddess. You have your own unique strength, and she needs that just as much as she needs our magic. So come, Ryber. Sleep and help heal Sirmaya."

"Yes," I said, voice firmer this time. I pushed through the pain that echoed in my skull, and I stood.

One crude step became two. Then six.

I reached Hilga, who smiled down at me. "You came just in time," she said. "There is space beside me."

It was true: between Tanzi and Hilga was a gap in the ice exactly my size. My Goddess had been waiting for me all along.

A matching smile split my face. I had made it. I had reached Sirmaya, I had reached the Sisters, and now we would sleep and help our Goddess heal.

That was what all the storms and earthquakes had meant. That was what all the black lines in the ice were.

When the sky splits and the mountain quakes,
Make time for good-byes,
For the Sleeper soon breaks.

Sirmaya was breaking—she was cleaving, and when she did, the world as we knew it would vanish. Of course I would give her what little power I had to keep that from happening.

Yet as I reached the hole meant for me, I glanced one last time at Tanzi.

And I stopped. Her eyes were open, huge and determined. She was not smiling. Her mouth worked and moved against an ice muffle.

Then the frost that silenced her crackled off. "No," she rasped. Then harder. "No, Ry. Don't do it."

"Tanz." I heaved toward her. My boots scratched over something; I didn't look down. I just pressed my hands against the ice.

Against my Threadsister. She was so close, yet out of reach.

"Listen to me, Ry." Each word Tanzi said seemed to take great focus, great strength. "You can still . . . live. You don't have . . . to be here."

"But I want to."

"Freedom, Ry. It takes . . . all . . . my force of will to reverse this ice long enough to speak to you. I wish I had never stepped inside the mountain, but you . . . You don't have to. Walk away, Ry. Save Sirmaya from beyond—" She broke off as a shard of ice scraped downward.

It clamped over her left eyelid, forcing it shut.

"No, no, no." I grabbed at the ice. Tried to heave it back up.

"Leave it," Tanzi said, voice strained. "Listen to your Lazy Bug."

I ignored her. Any exultation I had felt before was lost now. Replaced by the need to free Tanzi.

She didn't want to be here. I saw it in her eyes—her silver, silver eyes. I had to get her out.

Behind me, Hilga shouted, "No! Leave her, Ryber! You must sleep now!"

Meaningless words. I yanked harder at the ice.

"It won't work," Tanzi gritted out, and somehow, though all the

Sisters shrieked at me, her voice rang the clearest. "It's too late for me, Ry, but not for you. The Rules were never rules, don't you see? Too much time alone, and we lost ourselves—"

"No," I snarled. "No, no, *no*, Tanz." Yank, rip, yank.

The ice wouldn't budge, and Goddess—Tanzi's face was so cold. It was as another slice crawled down and snapped her right eye shut, that a sharp heat ignited in my foot.

I finally glanced down. A thousand pieces of shattered steel met my eyes.

My knife.

Just like that, I gave up. All fight drained from me in a single, downward swoop. If steel could not break this ice, then my fingers certainly never would. A choking sob gathered in my chest. I sagged into Tanzi.

Behind me, Hilga still shouted, "Hurry, Ryber! Get into the ice! Hurry!"

"Don't," Tanzi insisted. She shouted too, but her words were so tight. Pained, even. "We are not enough to heal her, Ry. Her magic is being used up too fast. But there is another way—"

Ice clawed over Tanzi's mouth. She choked. Sputtered.

She wasn't the only one. All of the Sisters broke off. All of them were now fully sealed in the ice.

And all I could do was lean against the ice and cry.

Useless. Helpless. I'd come so far, only to find this.

I was too late.

My family was in the ice for sleeping, and there was nothing I could do except join them. I could finally be like everyone else and sleep. Unless . . .

Unless I didn't.

There is another way. That was what Tanzi had said.

All of us, the Sisters and beyond, we existed because Sirmaya slept and dreamed at the very heart of our world.

A world I'd never actually seen, filled with people like Captain and Dirdra and the Threadwitch and all those Nubrevnans on the shore. If there was a way to keep them alive—to keep the world from ending—could I truly step into the ice and hope my power was enough to heal the Goddess?

No.

The answer was no.

Perhaps, all those years ago, I had not found my way to the Sorrow to join the Sisters, but rather, I had found my way there to save them.

"Ah," came a gentle rasp. My head jerked up.

It was Tanzi. A sliver of her mouth was still exposed, and somehow she had opened her eyes behind the ice.

She smiled then, crooked and restricted, but so Tanzi. So perfect.

"Silver eyes really suit you," she said, and then the ice finished its swaddling. Her eyelids sank shut.

She slept.

---– ✳ –---

Y2787 D338

LATER

I did it. I entered the doorway and I reached the Rook King's court atop Sirmaya's mountain.

Nadya waited in the cavern and watched me go. "May Sirmaya protect you," she whispered.

Then my feet crossed the threshold, and I was sucked into a blizzard made of fire. A burst of such intense power that it both scalded and froze at once. It sucked the air from my lungs and flipped my stomach straight into my skull. I felt stretched. I felt crushed. I felt made of starlight and molten stone.

Then, in a blink, it was over. I was *there*. In the matching doorway Saria had carved on the cliffside above the Rook King's palace.

At this high an altitude, there was no escaping the sun—nor its fierce glare upon the snow. Worse, my legs collapsed beneath me from the sudden sense of weight. Of existence. Of mountain cold to gust against me.

Footsteps crunched on the snow, and then a warm weight dropped over me. It smelled of tallow and wool. "These will protect your eyes," came the Rook King's low voice, and I felt his hands slide around my head.

A strap tightened, and tentatively I opened one eye. *Horsehair goggles*, I realized, and when I tipped up my chin, I saw that the Rook King wore a matching pair. With the hood of his black cloak towed up against the wind, the only part of his face that showed was a grin.

"You did it," he said. "Well done."

I nodded, a breathy laugh falling from my tongue as he helped me rise. "I *did*, didn't I?" My words puffed with steam. "I built the door, Your Majesty, and here I am. I cannot believe it worked."

"I can." He offered me his arm and waved to a path cleared down the mountain's snowy side. "Will you join me? As I said in my last message, the general wishes to discuss defense of the doorways with you."

I nodded with far too much excitement. I had been ready for months to confer directly with the general, and I'd already told Nadya that it might be several hours before I returned.

"Let us go," I declared, and I allowed the King to guide me into the evergreens. His rook, which I hadn't noticed skulking in the trees, flapped over and settled on the King's shoulder.

I still didn't like that bird. It was far too human-like in its gaze.

We tromped past snowdrifts tucked behind stone walls, built just for that purpose, and we wove left and right around branches bowed low beneath the white. Not once did the wind stop its howl, and despite my added layer, I shivered and shook.

We had cold at the Convent, but this was a new level. Colder even than the deepest corners of Sirmaya's underground.

I had visited this mountaintop fortress once before, but it had been late spring then. The snow had not lain thick across the crags and peaks, and the people had not been mounds of shapeless wool with only horsehair goggles to reveal them as human.

Each person we passed in the woods bobbed at the knees and tapped their fur-covered brows with a mittened hand. The Rook King always returned the gesture, an aura of absolute respect rolling off him.

Gone was the sense of outsider. Here, in his own realm, the Rook King felt as he had when I'd first met him: a man who wanted to stop the ceaseless death caused by Exalted Ones unchecked. A man who loved his home and his people.

Down, down we zigged and zagged toward his dark palace on the cliff. The wind carried the sound of soldiers and horses in training: the clash of metal, the jangle of tack, and hundreds of voices—women's and men's—shouting as they worked.

The Rook King's army was the smallest of all the Paladins', but no one doubted his was the fiercest. Trained in this harshest of lands, his soldiers were led not only by the King, but also by a general known across the Witchlands as the best of the best.

He was, aside from the Sightwitch Sisters, the only person on the continent who knew what the Six intended, and though it had irked me to go all these years without an introduction, I was too giddy over the door to care today.

We crossed a low drawbridge slatted over a moat filled with snow. Yet we did not pass through the main gate. Instead, we skirted the yard, using a corner tower to reach the battlements.

There, I had a view of the soldiers in practice—and what a sight to behold. I will never forget it. Two hundred people, bundled up and layered in loose, leather armor, moved in perfect coordination at the bellowed cries of a man on a wooden scaffolding. He paced back and forth, dressed no differently from his subordinates.

The general, I presumed.

Crossing the battlements, we entered a private study, where a welcome fire snapped in the fireplace. Steaming, rosemary-scented broth waited on a short table at the room's center, and four cushions rested around it.

The King's bird swept off his shoulder and landed on a hook overlooking a long, curved desk covered in maps and letters.

"This is the general's office," the King explained, yet before he could peel off his goggles, the door creaked open.

A fur-covered head poked in, and a decidedly feminine voice said, "Your Majesty, we need you at the stables, sir."

Instantly, the rook was off his perch and flapping back onto the King's shoulder. The sound of his flight drowned out whatever the woman said next—and whatever the King answered—yet the sudden stiffening of the King's spine told me it could not be good.

"I'll be right there," he told the woman. Then he swung his gaze back to me. His expression was inscrutable behind the wool and fur. "I need to go to the stables. We've had disease hit my favorite hounds. Lady Saria just arrived to help, and . . . I apologize, Sister Eridysi. Can you speak with the general alone?"

I bowed my head. "Of course."

"Thank you. I will join the two of you soon." And with that, he yanked on his goggles and pushed back into the winter's day.

The door thunked shut, and I was alone. After hanging my cloak and goggles on a knob by the door, I crossed to the fireplace to wait.

As I warmed up, a grin eased over my face. My head lolled back.

I had done it. *I had done it!* One passage was complete, and the remaining five would be easily done. Then, once we had them all, we could start porting people away from the Exalted Ones. Even the blade to kill them was almost complete too. All our plans were coming together.

I beamed so broadly my cheeks hurt. Even when the door rushed open and footsteps stomped inside, even as I turned to face whoever it might be, I still grinned.

I couldn't help it.

The general stopped dead in his tracks at the sight of me, the door open and his mittened hand clutching the latch. Snow swooped in. Cold washed against me.

My smile faltered. Then frosted away entirely. Why did he stare? Why did he not shut the door?

I offered a polite bow. "I am Sister Eridysi. You must be the general."

He flinched. Then, voice muffled by the angle and the layers, he mumbled, "Yes."

Aiming for a string of hooks nearby, his back to me, he removed each layer. Hat, scarf, leather armor, outer coat, undercoat.

He shrank and shrank and shrank, until at last there was nothing but a man with dark hair and a standard black silk uniform.

Then he turned to face me.

"You," I breathed.

"You," was his reply. Then his gaze dropped to his toes, and he scrubbed a hand over his dark hair.

Nervous. He was . . . nervous.

"You told me you were a soldier." Accusation laced my tone.

He offered a tight laugh. "An advanced soldier." Then he shrugged, his eyes finally lifting to meet mine across the room. "Does . . . it matter?"

"No!" I rushed forward two clumsy steps. Then stopped, feeling a fool.

Now I was the one staring uncomfortably at the ground. "I simply . . . That is to say, I assumed you were somewhere near the Convent. In one of the Rook King's southern forts."

"A fair guess." He cleared his throat. "I never specified."

"You must truly love the girls." I twirled away and marched to his desk. It was so much easier to speak when I didn't face him.

So much easier to breathe.

"Not that I doubted you loved them, of course," I rambled on. "But it must take you an entire day to travel both ways."

"*Each* way," he corrected. "The journey takes two days."

I watched him from the corner of my eye as he approached me at the desk.

He frowned. Then he was at the table and standing beside me. Close enough that I could smell iron and horse. Close enough that, if I wanted to, I could have reached out and touched him.

"So you are *that* Sightwitch. The inventor without the Sight."

Shame gusted over me.

"Your eyes are silver," he continued, oblivious of the fire raging on my cheeks. "So I assumed you were like the others."

"Well, I'm not," I said flatly.

Now he was the one to blurt. "I meant no offense. I'm sorry, my lady. Truly."

I believed him and forced a smile. "I suppose we're both more than we let on."

"Ah." The worried lines of his face smoothed away and he offered me one of his own smiles. The kind that made his bright eyes crinkle and my stomach knot tight. "When did you get here?"

"Only moments ago. The first doorway is complete." I gestured vaguely up the mountain. "I just tested it."

He stiffened. "*You* tested it?"

"Of course. Who else would?"

"I don't know. Someone who isn't you." He shook his head, an impatient movement. "What if the magic had gone wrong? What if you had not arrived here at all? Did you even try it before you stepped through?"

"How would I possibly try it?" I drew back my shoulders.

"Throw a stone in it."

"The spell only works on the living."

"Then send a Paladin!"

"Oh, right," I retorted, "because the most important people in all the land would risk their lives testing my doorway."

"Yes! And they should! This is their rebellion—"

"This is *our* rebellion!"

"—and if they die, then they'll be reborn!"

"Why are you shouting at me?"

"Because it was foolish! What if you had *died*?"

"The Six would have gone on just fine without me," I snipped, and because I didn't know what else to do—because I don't like confrontation—I gathered myself up to my fullest height and said, "I will tell Lisbet and Cora you send your love. Good day, General."

Then I stalked past him and aimed for the door. As I grabbed at my cloak, ready to yank it off its hook, his voice skated over me. The words were too low to discern.

"What?" I angled back.

He cleared his throat. Then louder, he offered, "They aren't the only reason."

"Who?"

"The girls."

I released the cloak. Then turned to stare at him straight on.

There was no more anger to cloud his eyes. Nor pain nor anything else I could easily recognize.

Then he repeated, "The girls aren't the only reason I come each full moon," and I knew exactly what expression he wore.

Need.

And I needed it too. I had all along, hadn't I? Since that day at the Sorrow when the world had tilted sideways. When he'd flashed a single smile.

I would not let this moment slip past.

In four long steps I was back to him. Rolling onto my toes and looping my fingers behind his head.

His hair was as soft as I had dreamed it would be.

Then our lips touched, and it was over. I had kissed before. A hundred girls around me, and I was bound to try. But I'd never met someone who made me want to keep kissing like he did.

Twice, I had to pull back to catch my breath. The room spun. His face spun.

But I could not stay away for long. A heartbeat, perhaps two, and then our lips were crushed together once more.

This was it. This was what it was all about—this was true Sight, true understanding of what life really meant.

The general and his daughters had been the change to shake me loose, and I knew that from this moment on, I would never be the same.

I knew what I had to do. It was what Tanzi wanted me to do, what she'd wanted me to do all along.

To go beyond.

To be free.

All these hours and days and weeks, I had had only one purpose: to reunite with my Sisters and my Lazy Bug.

All these years, I'd thought this was my future. I would become a powerful Sightwitch Sister and join the ranks of those who protected Sirmaya—and who one day joined with her forever in sleep.

But my Goddess was dying. If I finally took hold of what I'd always wanted, it would mean turning my back on a world that needed me.

I couldn't do that, and Captain had been right all along. Back on the Way Below, he'd been right: there was not one set path for me. I could choose another. I could make my own Sight with clarity and purpose and thinking beyond.

Tanzi had said there was another way to heal Sirmaya, so I would find it.

I splayed my fingers on the ice, right over Tanzi's heart. It was so silent now. So still. "I'll come back for you," I whispered. "I'll heal the Sleeper, and you'll wake up again."

Then I gathered up Eridysi's diary and the gold leather pouch, and with my chin held high, I left behind all the people I'd ever loved.

The ice, however, had a different plan in mind. I reached the exit, ready to march back into the main spiral, when a loud *crack!* rattled through the room. Everything shook, hard enough to topple me.

I found my gaze level with Trina's. She looked so young within the ice.

Ice, I realized, that was moving. Too surprised to react, I watched as three crystals lanced out from beside Trina's head.

More cracking sounded around me, echoing and solid. I looked down to find ice rising up from the floor.

It wasn't until the ice slid its claws around me that I finally moved.

I bolted for the door. Ice erupted from all angles. Bigger, fiercer. Stalactites to pin me down.

This tomb did not want me to leave.

I dodged. I leaped. I hit the spiral pathway, where the Rook hovered in place, panic clear in his frantic wingbeats.

He saw me. He cawed. Then he folded his wings and dropped like a stone.

"Curse you!" I screeched, slinging left. "I can't *fly!*"

I couldn't blame him for leaving me, though, for as I launched my legs high, ice began to fall. A tremor from a dying—a *cleaving*—Goddess.

I ran.

I don't know how I mustered such speed after so much exhaustion. After losing the one thing I'd wanted: my family. Yet somehow, by the grace of Sirmaya, I ran faster than I ever had before.

The world around me misted into a streaming haze. Ice rocketed toward me, sentient and grabbing. I ducked, I dove, I twisted and turned. I hopped, I stumbled, I ran, ran, *ran*.

"I don't want to sleep!" I tried to holler between bounding steps. "I want to heal you! I'll find another way—no sleeping!"

The ice did not listen. The tremor did not stop.

I reached the bottom floor, where the Rook screeched and flapped at what little remained of the exit. If I'd thought it tight before, it was nothing compared to now. I wasn't sure I could even fit in there, much less squeeze all the way through.

The Rook squawked a warning.

I dove sideways. Half a beat later, ice smashed to the ground.

A huge column of it shattered outward, and as each shard hit the ground, it reached for me.

No. No. *No.* What little power I possessed was a drop of water compared to the other Sisters. Thousands of them slept in this mountain, from the thousands of years we'd been protecting Sirmaya. With my mind, my drive—I would heal the Goddess from the outside.

I would not succumb to the sleeping.

I hit the exit and flung myself inside. Cold wrought the air from my lungs, and ice razored into my chest, my legs. Shrinking! This space was shrinking! And the ice would not let go. Over and under, it crowded in, trying to hold me down.

"Release me!" I shoved sideways. Harder. Harder. Blood streaked the blue behind, but I couldn't stop. The Rook had squirmed ahead, and since he was still moving, there had to be a way out.

Time stretched into a strange, incongruous thing measured in grunts and cracks and endless straining. Until finally I was there—I could see a sliver of darkness that could only be Paladins' Hall.

As if sensing how near I was to escape, the ice closed in all the harder. A shackle sliced around my left wrist. Then another around my ankle.

I tugged, I fought, I screamed, "I don't want to sleep! I am going to heal you! Let me go!"

Still, the ice ignored me. It pulsed outward, a vise to clamp off my breath, to smash in my skull.

Still, I battled and reached. Blood and tears mingled in my mouth. There was the hall—right there. I was so close, so close.

I reached it.

Even now as I write this, I do not know how. The ice moved enough for me to free my wrist and ankle, then I toppled headfirst through the doorway.

But I wasn't safe yet, for the ice was not stopping at the door. It was thrumming outward, trying to claim me even as the door's halves swung in.

Please shut, please shut.

The door did not shut, and in a stone-trembling roar, the ice burst out. It was coming for me.

I scrabbled around, my mind a clash of rules and fruitless prayers. Rule 35: Stay calm, for panic serves no one.

Please, Sleeper, help me. Please, please.

Rule 13: Never leave a fire untended.

"Enough," I hissed at myself. "Focus, focus." What were my options? I was alone on the ledge with the Rook nowhere to be seen— nor Captain. I hadn't thought he would be here, but I'd hoped.

How else was I going to leave this platform? Even without the ice, I needed a way off.

Fighting to ignore the approaching ice—so loud, so loud—I scuttled to the edge of the stone and stared down.

A galaxy of stars met my eyes.

We had flown right over it, and I'd never seen.

As I stared at the stars—not true stars, but spirit swifts swirling and dancing amid nine lights placed in perfect coordination—I realized that the answer stared up at me.

I laughed then. The sound burbled out, a pot boiling over in my belly.

For it was right there. The answer to the Nine Star Puzzle was right there and had been all along.

Suddenly, I knew what Tanzi had been saying all these years. *Think beyond, Ryber. Think beyond.*

She meant beyond the framework of stars. I had always assumed that I had to keep my chalk inside the slate, but it wasn't true— nothing in the instructions ever said I had to.

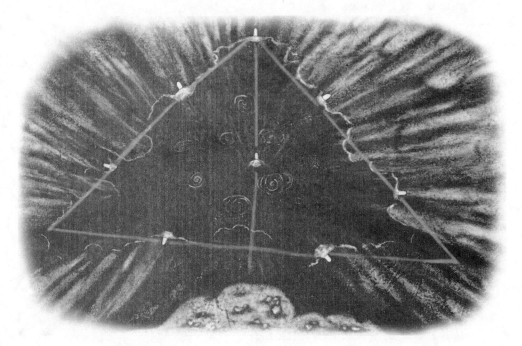

I tore out my map, and there, right under my nose, was my second answer: the way off this ledge. It was even scribbled on the paper.

Palladin's Hall, 38.

38: THE RULE OF DISPUTED TRUTH
Oftentimes, Memory Records will offer different accounts for the same event. As such, all Memory Records are true and all Memory Records are false, for what is life except perception?

It's what all these numbers on the map were. *Rules.* But I'd been so trapped inside the framework, I hadn't thought to think beyond.

Tanzi had recognized that the stars, the Rules—none of it was real. It was only what we chose them to be.

I stuffed the map into Eridysi's diary, no time to fold it. The ice was at my heels, and I had to go. Now.

I threw a final glance down. If I was wrong, then it was a long way to fall—a very long way to fall.

But I wasn't wrong.

This was my true path. One without structure, without Sight or guarantee or anyone at my side to help me forge ahead. Yet I knew what mattered most, and I would do whatever it took to get there.

Just as I had found the Supplicant's Sorrow all alone as a child, I would find a way to heal the Goddess. And when Sirmaya was healed, when her sleep was calm and there was no more risk that this world would end, then I would return for my Sisters. I would return for Tanzi.

And with that purpose held tight in my mind, I stepped off the ledge.

NUBREVNAN ROYAL SOIL BOUND & NAVY

Voicewitches

FOR: First Mate Stacia Sotar
FROM: His Royal Highness Merik Nihar

MESSAGE:

I have arrived at the border. Temporary Captain Kullen Ikray is still missing. Send more soldiers and supplies.

Also, we need new plans for the watchtowers. If one storm could decimate the structure, then what will happen when the Truce ends and war begins? Tell Vivia to get our engineers on it right away.

This message was recorded by Voicewitch Hermin Layhar in Lovats , sent by Voicewitch Ginna Tritza in northern Nubrevnan border , on the 216 day in the 18th year since the signing of the Twenty Year Truce.

I did not fall to my death. The bridge had been there all along, even if I could not see it. What is life except perception?

This was how Tanzi had lived. While I'd been hiding behind my walls and rules, she had tasted freedom.

I walked and walked, the bridge ever descending while starry spirit swifts glimmered closer with each step.

The doorway that Captain had taken hazed into focus. First a glowing wave of blue. Then the archway. Rubble. Jungle vines.

And finally the Rook, waiting for me on the floor.

When at last my feet stepped onto visible stone once more, my lungs whooshed an exhale of such force that I doubled over. Then I laughed again, the same delight singing through me that I had felt above the invisible bridge.

My jubilance was short-lived, though, for as I drew myself up, I found the Rook chittering his beak. He skipped forward, backward, side to side.

He wanted me to go through the door.

I wiped at my face and fixed my gaze on the jungle fanning ahead. Sweat, blood, a salty line of tears—all of it smeared onto my sleeve, but I hardly noticed. My thoughts were on the Rook.

He had guided me and saved me every inch of the way. He'd saved Captain too.

"It's him, isn't it?" I asked, trudging a step closer to the door. "He's a Paladin?"

The Rook's head bobbed. He clacked his beak.

"And he's important."

Another clack, and this time the Rook ruffled his feathers. "Hurry," he was saying. "No time."

I wanted to ask why. I wanted answers to *everything*—why Captain mattered, what waited beyond that door, and above all, how to heal Sirmaya. But the Rook couldn't speak, and my only chance for real answers lay beyond that rubble.

My gaze flicked down to Eridysi's diary, still clenched in one hand. Perhaps it held answers too. After all, I had found this for a reason, and there were no coincidences, right?

"Will I be able to get back in?" I asked the Rook, lifting my gaze once more.

Another bird nod, and a tension unwound in my chest. I could return. I could fetch Captain, and we could return.

"And . . . will you go with me through the door?"

His head shuddered with a no.

"All right, then," I murmured. I hadn't really thought he would, and now he was clucking at me to hurry. So after easing the diary and pouch onto the rubble, I clambered over the fallen bricks and swept aside the vines.

Then, for the first time in my living memory, I left the grounds of the Convent.

— ✳ —

Y2788 D3

MEMORIES

All the doors are finished. Tomorrow, we will move the first people through. They will come from the Scorched Lands, for Rhian is the only one of the Six with a network in place. The Exalted Ones watch too closely everywhere else.

But it's a start. Person by person, family by family, we will move them into our secret city. A temporary home to hold them, hidden and safe, until we can find more permanent lands. Until the Six can use my now-finished blade to kill the Exalted Ones once and for all.

Something Lisbet said, though, has left me pacing and picking my nails to the quick. It was as I celebrated with her father and Cora in the workshop. We had mulled wine. I had been saving the spices for weeks.

We were giddy. The heat from the drink had given us all flushed faces, and the excitement from finishing the last door—we laughed and laughed and I felt more full than I had ever felt in my life.

A true gift from the Goddess.

I stirred a fresh pot of wine while Cora taught her father to play taro. Lisbet had come to my side, watching as the liquid spun and spun in its pot. The serene smile she always wore rested on her small mouth.

Then it suddenly stretched bigger, her eyes glowing bright, and she said, "I always wanted a brother."

"Oh?" was my absent reply. It was such an odd, Lisbet-like thing to say.

But then she patted at my stomach. "Him," she said emphatically. "Though I won't get to meet him for a very, very long time."

It took three circles of the spoon before I understood what she'd said. "You mean . . ." My stirring slowed to a stop. "I am with child?"

She nodded, and I gulped. Her words simply would not click into place.

Me. A mother by blood.

There was no time for this revelation to settle, though, before Lisbet moved on to the next subject.

"It will all be over quickly, Dysi, so you don't need to worry like you do."

"What will?" The question was breathy and lost. "The child?"

"No. I mean the end."

Cold ran through me. "The end of what, Lis?"

"Of everything, of course. It will be painful, but I promise it won't last long . . . Oh, the wine is burning!" She pointed to the pot, and before I could stop her, she'd snatched the spoon and taken over.

It took all my energy to feign joy after that, and as I have done with all of Lisbet's prophecies, I scribbled down these words on the nearest page I could find—a page already filled with her visions.

I should ask Nadya to search the scrying pool for answers, but I find myself bound by chains. Unable to leave the workshop, unable to do anything but circle the same path as blood wells from nailbeds torn too low.

I did not tell the general of our child. I should have, but I am too scared.

The Paladins we locked away will one day walk among us. Vengeance will be theirs, in a fury unchecked, for their power was never ours to claim. Yet only in death, could they understand life. And only in life, will they change the world.
—Y2786 D267

It will all be over quickly. The end of everything.
—Y2786 D38

———— ✳ ————

I had no idea where in the Witchlands I was. When I strode through the doorway, fire had consumed me—or perhaps it had been cold. I couldn't tell. It was all so fast, so intense.

Then I was there. Somewhere *other*, where rain slashed and thunder boomed. Tree varieties I'd only seen sketched in books bent and creaked against a storm.

Cypress and salt cedar trees were so much larger in person, and much, much more frightening when they were about to break.

I was soaked before I'd made it ten paces from the doorway. Small runoff rivers cascaded across my feet and into my boots. I wasn't sure where I was going, I simply aimed for the eye of the storm. The skittering charge in the air thickened and shimmered the nearer I approached.

Captain's magic drew me to him; I was a magnet slinging toward a lodestone.

Rain battered me. Winds surged behind, against, around. I fought on, until the jungle fell away to reveal a narrow spit of beach where waves rocked and dragged.

I'd never seen the ocean, yet there was no time to take it all in, for without the jungle's cover, the storm's force doubled.

Hail pelted down. I had to fling up my arms to block against it. Yet I'd found him. A cyclone swept around him, much too strong for me to cross.

More concerning, though, was the boat he held above his head.

A huge beast of a ship, like the Dalmottis used for trade. His winds kept it aloft, while lightning slashed and jagged around him. It hit the boat's planks, the sand, and even Captain.

I narrowed my eyes, straining to focus through the brilliant light and whipping sands.

That was when I saw them: men. An entire crew's worth, half of them crawling away while the other half ran as fast as the wind would let them.

Oh, Captain, what have you done? He had cleaved again—of that much I had no doubt. Yet he'd been able to come back, inside the mountain. Surely he could be saved again.

I certainly had to try, if for no other reason than to save the crew now trying to flee.

My arms fell. The hail beat into me anew, but this was nothing compared to the hell I'd faced inside the mountain. If I could face monsters in the Crypts and shadow wyrms, if I could battle Sirmaya's ice and come out alive, then a little storm was nothing to fear.

Sand scraped my face; lightning sizzled my cheeks. Then I was to the ship's shadow.

The boat jolted, dropping close. I fell to the sand. "Stop!" The word ripped from my throat and vanished on the wind. Even if I hadn't worn my throat raw while screaming in the ice, I could never produce enough sound for Captain to hear.

Yet as I dragged up from the sand, something dug into my hipbone. *The bell.* In a storm-torn instant, I was on my knees and wrenching the bell from its pouch. Then I swung that thing with all my might, directly at the sky. Directly at Captain.

The sound was neither pure nor loud, but it was enough. It rippled through me, more feeling than anything else.

Captain felt it too. Through the lashing sand and lightning, I saw him tense. Then roll his head back.

He wheeled around, the ship spinning with him and crashing lower, lower. Low enough for me to see barnacles and caulking, to hear cows' plaintive moaning from within.

Then a groan of wood, a smash of lightning, and Captain threw the boat. As easily as Tanzi skipped stones off the Sorrow, Captain launched the trade ship into the jungle.

I never saw it land. My attention was on the sailors, finally able to run. Soon, they were nothing more than shadowy specks beyond a wall of wind.

Captain stalked close. His skin roiled and shifted. Tarry lines pulsed beneath his pallid cheeks. His eyes were black from rim to rim.

But there was no violence in his posture. No death. He was puzzled more than anything else.

So I slung the bell again. Harder. No rhythm or beat, just a vicious clanging to holler above the storm.

Then, as Captain came toward me, I screamed the only words I could think of—words he'd sung to me before.

> "The maidens north of Lovats!
> None ever looked so fair!
> When they catch your eye, you'll fall in love,
> So everyone beware."

He stopped his approach. I did not stop mine. On and on, the bell rattled in my grasp, and on and on I hollered.

> "The maidens north of Lovats!
> Are as strong as ten large men,
> With minds as sharp as hammered steel,
> When they fight they always win."

He crumpled to his knees, and the winds answered in kind. Softer, softer they spun.

> "The maidens north of Lovats!
> If ever one you meet,
> Turn hide and run the other way,
> Or a blighter you will be!"

I sang the final line, and the pustules smoothed on Captain's face. The lines of tar shriveled and shrank.

I stopped ringing the bell, and as the last wind whispered away, the final shreds of darkness swirled into nothing. Familiar blue eyes met mine.

Then Captain bowed over, breath heaving, and rasped, "Thank you, Ryber. Thank you."

---- ✳ ----

Y2788 D41

MEMORIES

The Exalted Ones found us. They found the doors, and I fear the world is ending.

There is no time. The ice comes for me, and I must write. Lisbet *told* me I must write.

Five hundred and two people. That was all we got through the door from the Scorched Lands and into the underground city.

Then the Exalted Ones came. They used the door from the Windswept Plains—a door that none of us were guarding. The Six, the general, and I were too busy coordinating the movement of a hundred families through the cavern.

The only warning we had was a rumble through the earth. Saria felt it first. I saw her frown, then stride away from our spot at the rear of the group. "What is it?" I called after her.

Then the earthquake hit.

After that, my memory is a mess of broken moments. Of falling to my knees, then heat barreling over me—so hot, my hair caught fire and my eyebrows singed off.

Of screams, frightened and shrill, as people fled. A dropped satchel. A forgotten book.

Of the Exalted Ones loosing magic and war cries that hummed with fury, betrayal, revenge. Each emotion spilled over me. Solid. *Real*.

What had we unleashed?

Then I watched the Six abandon our group and meet the Exalted Ones head on.

In those seconds that seemed never to end, only two words filled my mind: *the girls*. Fool that I am, I had let them join us in the cavern. I'd sent them up to the highest ledge, beside the spiral tomb's entrance, where I'd thought they could watch everything proceed while safely out of reach.

Fool, fool, fool.

I had to get to them.

Then he was beside me, my Heart-Thread, clutching my arm to lift me from the stone. Together, we ran across the glamoured bridge that shook beneath our feet.

Wind roiled against us, water and ice sliced past—and fire, fire, everywhere there was fire.

But we did not stop. We did not slow. Hands grasped tight, we ran for the girls, who meant everything.

We reached the ledge. The girls were not there, but the tomb entrance was open, and Lisbet's knife poked from the key slot. Its amber hilt glinted in the flames.

Clever, clever Lisbet. We could hide in the tombs until the war below had ended.

I yanked the knife free and flung a final glance behind.

I wish I had never looked. The Six were losing. Rhian and Midne lay crumpled on the stones, while fire engulfed Bastien. Baile was pinned by swords to the wall, and Saria was trapped inside a growing cage of stone. The Rook King—the one to whom I had given the Paladin-blade for safekeeping—was nowhere in sight.

There was nothing to be done, not with the girls' safety at risk. So I hauled the door shut and led the way into the ice.

Our breaths hashed out, overloud. Our feet hammered and scraped. Until at last we reached the spiral's heart.

And there, my darling, wonderful girls awaited. Lisbet stood tall, her sister clutched tight. Her eyes glowed.

Once to them, their father fell to his knees to inspect them all over.

Lisbet rooted her brilliant gaze on me, though. "We must sleep now, Dysi."

It took me a moment to understand what she meant. Sleeping was what dying sisters did when they saw their time come.

"No, Lisbet." I cupped her face. "We can hide in the tomb, but once this battle is over, we will leave."

"But it won't end. He's betrayed them all, don't you see?" She pulled from my grasp and turned to her father. "Tell her, Da. Tell her that it's time to sleep now."

"Sleep?" He glanced to me, confused. "Lis, love, we need to hide. Like Dysi said."

"No." Cora pulled free from her father's grip, and slipping her little fingers into Lisbet's, she drew her sister away three paces. Then both girls thrust out their jaws.

"Lisbet saw what is to come," Cora said, "and we have to sleep now. All of us—even you, Da, so you can be there when she wakes up." Cora pointed at me. Then up the spiral. "There's a tomb waiting for us."

Their father rose. "I don't understand."

"I do." The words slippered from my throat, for I *did* understand. This was what Lisbet had seen.

And this was what Sirmaya had chosen for us all.

"It won't hurt," Lisbet said to me. To her father: "The ice will protect us for a time, and then we'll sleep until it's time to wake up again."

My fingers moved to my belly. "What about . . . him, Lis?" I almost choked on the words. Tears slid down my face—when had those started?

"He'll be fine," Cora answered. "Lizzie told me all about him, and he's going to be a very good older brother one day."

"Older brother?" I tried to ask, but the girls were already marching for the spiral.

Their father did not follow.

"Come." I reached for him and took his hands in mine. He looked ancient in this light, and so tired. "You must trust the magic of the Goddess, my love."

Still he did not move. "There are people out there. I must help them."

"You can do nothing." I squeezed his fingers tightly. "The Exalted Ones will kill you."

"I have to try," he countered. "I cannot abandon my king."

"Yet you can abandon me? And the girls?"

His eyes averted. "No. I . . ." Then he wilted into me, his forehead resting against mine. "We cannot walk away from this, Dysi. Some-one betrayed us."

"Or we were not careful enough."

"Da!" came Cora's call, muffled by the ice. A heartbeat later: "Dysi! Come! We have to hurry!"

"I don't want to do this," he murmured.

"I know. But you have to trust me and trust the girls." I rested my hands on either side of his face—that beautiful, lined face that I had grown to love. "This is what the Goddess wills, and so we must obey." Then, when he made no move to turn, I murmured the only No'Amatsi words I knew: "*Mhe verujta.*"

Trust me as if my soul were yours.

He gave a long, slow blink. Then whispered, "*Mhe verujta,*" and together we ascended the spiral.

A tomb waited for us with four gaps in the ice. If I'd had any doubt that Lisbet's vision was true, it was gone now.

Though that did not mean I was ready. Cora went first, then her father. And I cried—it was selfish of me, but I could not stop the tears.

Everything I had worked for had crumbled away. The doors, the rebellion, and a life with my Heart-Thread, these two little girls, and the boy growing in my womb.

I was the last into the ice, for Lisbet told me I must write a final entry. "Leave the diary and your taro cards behind," she ordered me. "The last Sister will need them."

Yet as the ice scuttled over Lisbet, I had to ask her. I had to know. "How can you be so calm? How have you lived all these weeks and months despite knowing all that was coming?"

"Not despite, Dysi." She gave me a sympathetic half smile, and it was not a child's face that stared at me. "*Because*. We value things more when we know they won't last forever."

Then ice covered her completely, and she joined her family in the Sleeper's embrace.

So I did as she commanded, and now it is only I to sit alone in this room of eternal cold and blue, blue, blue.

Whoever you are, last Sightwitch Sister, please make use of the time you have. Do not do as I did. Do not trap yourself away inside a mountain with your head stuffed in the past.

You have a life to live, and Sirmaya thinks it is an important one.

So go outside. Meet the world and embrace its trials head-on.

A lone sister is lost, you know, so never let yourself be alone.

---- ⁎ ----

Kullen Ikray
Y18 D218

Ryber tells me that I must write everything now that I remember it.
"Nothing is real until you record it," she insists, and though she laughs
at my poor handwriting, I do as she commands.

She is not the sort of woman to be disobeyed. *Your smile is terrifying.*
Not that I would ever want to. Her frown is quite terrifying. *Your smile is nice.*

My name is Kullen Ikray, though Ryber still calls me Captain. I
was a Captain, temporarily, and at the urging of my Threadbrother
Merik, I led a crew of sailors and civilians to the northern border of
Nubrevna. We were building watchtowers, and all was progressing
with perfection.

Until it wasn't. I received word about a possible Dalmotti tradesman willing to negotiate with Nubrevnans. Well, specifically with *me*.
I decided not to tell Merik. After all, he is a prince and he has more
than enough to worry about. I could fly down to this rendezvous
point and be back in a day.

I should have known, Ry. I should have known it was a trap. How
did this Dalmotti know where to find me? How did he know who
I was to begin with? But the prospect of food and trade clouded all
judgment. I left immediately, and though my lungs protested at the
demands of a flight without breaks, I crossed all the way to the coast
in a single day.

I met the tradesman on the shore. He had two ships, one on which
he had sailed and another packed with food and livestock. Mine for
the taking if I would just give him the one thing he wanted.

Me.

He wanted *me*, and though I plied him with the wares of Nubrevna (we have excellent sheep), he grew more and more insistent.

Then he turned on me completely and attacked. He and thirteen of his men. I am an excellent fighter, Ry, but even I cannot take on that many trained sailors. I had to use my magic, and for the first time in my life, I had to use it to cause harm. Without aim, without focus, I had to blast my winds crudely and try to flee.

Stop bragging

But when an arrow hit me . . . That was when everything shifted. In a haze, I flew ashore and found my way through the jungle. Somehow, I discovered that door and entered the mountain.

I don't remember what came next. Not clearly. All I recall with any clarity is you. I woke up, frozen to my core, and there you were.

I thought you were either a ghost or goddess. Luckily, you were neither. I *would* call you a goddess, but I know you'll just scowl and tell me to shove off. *Shove off.* Sorry. Although I do like that you're smiling now.

I don't know if the arrow wound or the magic of the mountain rattled my brains, but I forgot who I was or how I'd gotten there. It wasn't until I returned to the jungle that my memories came back.

The sailors and tradesman came back too. I would have thought they'd have left me to die, but there they were, combing the beach in search of me. When they found me, the arrows hit me in quick succession.

After that . . . I really don't remember. I lost all control. Heat took over. It throbbed inside me, and I was hungry—so *blighted* hungry.

But then you saved me. Clanging a bell and singing a shanty, you brought me back from the edge.

I owe you everything, Ryber Fortsa. My life, my mind, my—

That's enough of that. This is for facts, not feelings

But I like feelings. And you're smiling even bigger now, which I also like.

Only because you're funny to look at.

Ouch.

——— ✳ ———

Ryber Fortiza

Y18 D223 — 49 days since I became the last
Sightwitch Sister

MEMORIES

~~Captain~~ Kullen left me today. With his wounds fully healed, his
memory returned, and even his uniform scrubbed clean, there was
nothing left to keep him here.

We sat on that boulder by the grassy knoll that overlooks the falls.
Even the Rook had joined us, though he seemed more interested in
bathing himself than watching the river below.

Nubrevnans crawled across the forest, the shore. At least a hundred women and men, and with one angry Windwitch at the fore.

"Merik," Kullen informed me, "acting like he always does. He will
budget and ration, even to the detriment of his own health . . . *until*
I'm involved. Then he will waste a hundred sailors and witches and
boats and food."

"It's what Thread-family does," I said quietly.

Something in my tone must have betrayed my thoughts, for Kullen's brows pinched, and he offered a gentle smile. "I'm sorry about
the Sisters."

I pretended not to hear, and in my most Hilga-like, matter-of-fact
manner, I got to my feet, dusted off my tunic, and declared, "There's
something I need to tell you."

He winced. "That sounds ominous."

"When you leave the glamour"—I gestured south—"you'll forget everything that happened here. The memories will get buried in a place you cannot find them."

His eyebrows shot high. Then, in a flurry of limbs and speed, he hauled to his feet. "I'll forget *everything*? Even you?"

I nodded.

"I didn't forget when I left Paladins' Hall. On the beach, I remembered you!"

"Because the glamour doesn't reach inside the mountain."

"But I don't want to forget you, Ryber. Or . . . anything that's happened. Please—can't you change the spell?"

"No." I twisted away to frown in the Rook's general direction. I knew this would not go well, yet it was turning out harder than I'd imagined.

Because *I* didn't want him to forget me either.

I hopped off the boulder, and grass blades scratched at my knees.

Kullen followed, leaping down in a graceful whip of wind. His shadow stretched long over the meadow.

"Is this why you made me write down what I remembered? You knew I would forget."

"Hye," was all I said before striding to the falls' edge.

The Rook paused his cleaning to watch me stalk his way with Kullen fast on my heels.

"Then I won't leave," Kullen said, though it was less assertion and more plaintive beg. "I'll stay here—"

"And do what?" I cut in. "This is no place for you, and an entire army is trying to find you."

"A navy," he murmured in a very ~~Captain~~ Kullen-like correction. Then, with sudden animation, he added, "You said 'buried.' That the memories would be 'buried in a place I cannot find them'—which means they'll still be in here. I just have to . . . to dig them up somehow."

"You won't be able to." It took all my control to keep my stern Hilga mask in place.

"I will," he insisted, and there was an edge to his voice I'd never heard before. A determination—a strength that could tame storms and summon cyclones.

"It's time," I said, motioning to the falls. To the river below. "You need to go before some Nubrevnan accidentally finds this place and I'm forced to kill him."

He sniffed, a bitter sound. "You would never follow through with Rule 37." He strode to the cliff's edge, and though he scowled down at the sailors and ships, I do not think he truly saw them.

"Will we ever meet again?" he asked eventually, dragging his gaze back to mine.

I hesitated. There was one side of Lady Fate's knife, one path that I could take in which I was certain we would meet again. The answers to healing Sirmaya might reside somewhere in that Paladin mind of his, meaning one day I would need to find him.

And if I was being honest, I wanted to find him.

But there is always the sharp, hidden side of Lady Fate's knife, where what we want is not what we ultimately get.

"I . . . will try," I forced out, groping for the right words. Then I bobbed my head curtly and repeated, "I will try to find you. One day, Captain."

"Ah." His shoulders relaxed. A warm breeze gusted around us— not from the summer's day, but a charged wind. A happy wind.

Then Kullen flashed me his widest grin yet, and I couldn't help but match it with my own.

Either he was getting better at smiling, or I was getting used to it.

"Good-bye, Captain," I said with a small bow.

He lifted a fist to his heart and swept a bow so low that his pale head scraped across the grass. One bow for me, then a second for the Rook, who still splashed upon the shore.

"Safe harbors, Ryber Fortiza," he declared as fresh, magicked winds furled in. The grass lashed and waved. "And safe harbors to you, the Rook."

Then Kullen Ikray launched off the knoll, leaving me, the Convent, and his memories of us both far behind.

——— ✳ ———

Y18 D261 — 87 days since I became the last Sightwitch Sister

MEMORIES

The doorway to the underground city waited before me. Once I stepped through, I was *through*. There would be no easy return to the Convent. Unlike the other passages, this door had been created to go only one way. Refugees who'd entered the underground city could not return for safety reasons.

I felt bound to the stone, unable to move, just as I had for the past twenty-five drips of my new hourglass.

So much had changed since last I'd been in Paladins' Hall.

For one, I was finally clear-eyed, although I did not have the Sight like other Sisters. I still woke after dreamless nights, and I still slept after days in the Crypts with only ghosts to keep me company.

My eyes had silvered, I assumed, from being so close to the Goddess. Or perhaps because I had made a choice. I had chosen a path.

Skull-Face and the Death Maidens did not try to kill me anymore, though, so at least that was something.

Whatever those creatures were—strange extensions of ghostly memories or guardians created by Sirmaya Herself—I did not know. But now that my eyes were silver, they paid me no mind when I entered their darkened Crypts.

For two, the Rook had left me. Without warning or good-bye, he had flapped off the day after Kullen had departed, and I hadn't seen him since.

All I could think was that his master was out there somewhere. The Rook King. A Paladin with a fortress in the blustery, windy mountains that I'd read about in Eridysi's diary. Why the bird had lived all these centuries, why he had helped me in the mountain, I really could not guess—though certainly I tried.

For three, I knew at least some of the Paladins were alive and spread across the Witchlands. Maybe they remembered who they were, or maybe they did not. Perhaps, like Kullen, they simply needed a broken blade and shattered glass to trigger the memories from their past lives.

Either way, Kullen and the Paladins were important.

As were the Cahr Awen, that pair of witches who could heal the Wells and, I surmised, Sirmaya too.

I didn't know how it was all connected, but the answers were out there. Not hiding in a record in the Crypts nor waiting to be summoned from a scrying pool. Nor even hoping to be flipped from Eridysi's taro deck—which was *my* taro deck now.

With that thought, I couldn't resist snapping over three cards. One last peek at the future, to see what might be coming.

Yet all I got were the same cards I'd always drawn the last few days: The Paladin of Hounds, Lady Fate, the Giant.

Kullen. Me. Change.

I had spent almost an entire week in Eridysi's workshop, going over her inventions and notes. There was so much to be found! Little notes from Lisbet and Cora, perfectly preserved, as well as some of Lisbet's prophecies that had been overlooked when Sister Nadya and the rest had assembled everything into "Eridysi's Lament."

Which, of course, was Lisbet's Lament all along.

In the workshop, I learned about Threads and power and life before the Convent was cut off from the world, masked behind a glamour after the battle of the Twelve wrecked everything.

I learned that Tanzi was right: the rules were never meant to be Rules, but merely suggestions that we had added to and added to over the hundreds of years we'd been cut off. The Sisters, myself above all, had lived by the rules until they had caged us in.

With no change to shake us loose, we became lone Sisters gone lost.

I also learned about choice. Eridsyi had never been gifted with Sight, so she had made her own—just as I had done in the tomb and just as I was doing now.

You'll understand once you're Summoned? Well, I'd Summoned myself, and now I *did* understand: paths do not come to you. You have to find them for yourself, and sometimes, you have to carve new ones entirely.

That knowledge alone has given me power indeed.

Twisting my neck, I tossed a final glance to a tiny flicker of blue high atop the end of a hidden bridge.

This wasn't forever. I would be back for Tanzi and Hilga and the rest of my Thread-family. I would be back when magic was healed and Sirmaya was no longer dying.

"I love you, Lazy Bug," I said. Then I pivoted back to the door.

It was time. I was ready, and before another drop of quicksilver could fall, I steeled my spine and walked out of the Convent, out of the mountain, and into my new life.

I was the last Sightwitch Sister, and I had work to do.

Tanzi Lamanaya
Y17 D319

Threadsisters

The Sleeping Giant

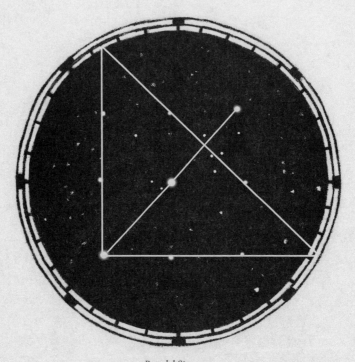

Rtes dol Sirmaya
The Weapon of the Giant that Cradles Us When We Sleep

A recent excavation at an early Marstoki fortress in the Sirmayan Mountains revealed a shrine beneath the primary structure. Inside and perfectly intact was a relief of the Sleeping Giant constellation with the words *Rtes dol Sirmaya* underneath. Sirmaya, a deity worshipped by the earliest humans to inhabit the Witchlands, roughly translates into "The Giant That Cradles Us When We Sleep," while *Rtes dol* means "the weapon of."

Overtop the stars were remnants of painted lines, mostly eroded by the ebb of time, a bow-like shape made across the constellation as well as across six adjacent stars.

ACKNOWLEDGMENTS

For the Witchlanders: you all continue to be the reason I write this series. I think of you every time I hit a sticky spot. "What would the Witchlanders want? What would they think?" So thank you for being my muse, my audience, and my friends.

Thank you to Rhys Davies and Heather Saunders for the amazing design and illustrations. You two were so patient, so attentive to detail, and so incredible at bringing the world of *Sightwitch* to life. Thank you, thank you.

Huge thanks to my wifey extraordinaire, Rachel Hansen. The Witchlands wouldn't be the Witchlands without your input, ideas, and constant calm in the face of my endless panic. *Tu me manques.*

To Melody Simpson and Sam Smith: I owe you eternal gratitude. Your feedback on *Sightwitch* was not only invaluable for the story, but it gave me, personally, a new lens through which to view the world.

Thank you to Melissa Lee and Cait Listro, whose cheerleading and critiques took this story (and my bruised ego) up a level. You each have a special spot in the Witchlands (pick a kingdom, any kingdom!).

Alex Bracken, Erin Bowman, Victoria Aveyard, Leigh Bardugo: I rely on you ladies so much. From real talk to craft talk, from venting to celebrating, you've been there for me. Thank you.

To Sébastien: I have no words to express my appreciation. Without you, I simply could not write books. You're my best friend, my

Heart-Thread, and my ever-willing partner in hilarious hijinks. *Je t'aime.*

Eternal thanks must go to Joanna Volpe, Devin Ross, and Hilary Pecheone, who have held my hand this past year . . . and every year. The whole New Leaf Literary gang has given me more support and love than I ever deserved. Thank you.

The same goes to my incredible team at Tor Teen: Alexis Saarela, Amy Stapp, Patty Garcia, Kathleen Doherty, Zohra Ashpari, Tom Doherty, Jim Kapp, Elizabeth Curione, Rafal Gibek, Cynthia Merman, Seth Lerner, Scott Grimando, Lucille Rettino, Theresa Delucci, Sumiya Nowshin, Rebecca Yaeger, Lauren Brantley, Megan Barnard, Alex Cameron, Jeremy Pink, and Megan Kiddoo. Thank you all so very much for all your hard work.

Last but never least, thank you to Whitney Ross. Advocate, editor, friend. I owe everything in this series to you and all you do behind the scenes. I am so, so glad the Witchlands brought us together, and here's to many more years of this awesome partnership.

ABOUT THE AUTHOR

SUSAN DENNARD has come a long way from small-town Georgia. Working in marine biology, she got to travel the world—six out of seven continents, to be exact (she'll get to Asia one of these days!)—before she settled down as a full-time novelist and writing instructor. She is the author of the Something Strange and Deadly series, as well as the Witchlands series, including the *New York Times* bestselling *Truthwitch* and *Windwitch*. When not writing, she can be found hiking with her dogs, slaying darkspawn on her Xbox, or earning bruises at the dojo.

Visit her on the web at
susandennard.com
thewitchlands.com
Twitter at @stdennard
Facebook at facebook.com/SusanDennardAuthor
susandennard.com/newsletter
stdennard.tumblr.com
instagram.com/stdennard

ABOUT THE ILLUSTRATOR

RHYS DAVIES is a freelance illustrator, mapmaker, and artist. Originally from Wales, Rhys studied fine art in London before moving to the United States. After spending many years as a product designer with Yankee Candle, Rhys now spends most of his time illustrating maps for novels, amongst other numerous creative projects. He lives in Amherst, Massachusetts, with his wife and two children.

Visit him on the web at
rhysspieces.com